THE HEALER

THE MESSES SERIES, BOOK TWO

KIERSTEN MODGLIN

Cover Design by Kiersten Modglin
Copy Editing by Three Owls Editing
Formatting by Kiersten Modglin
Copyright © 2018 by Kiersten Modglin.
All rights reserved.

First Print and Electronic Edition: 2018
kierstenmodglinauthor.com

To anyone who is still standing after their worst day. Keep fighting.
I'm rooting for you.

ONE

JESSE

"Time of death, twenty-two forty-five." Jesse Mathis stepped back from the operating table, pulling down the paper mask from his mouth and heaving a sigh. Cool tears collected in his eyes but he blinked them away, pulling the bloody gloves from his hands.

Her blood was all around him, on his surgical gown, beneath his feet. He could feel small specks of it drying on his face.

"Close her up, Donovan," he told the intern across from him. He nodded, his face solemn. Jesse wondered briefly if it was the first patient Donovan had lost. He couldn't remember. Or he didn't know. It didn't matter—they all hurt the same.

He stepped back through the heavy door, unable to catch his breath.

"Jesse?" Quinn's voice rang out from behind him, the concern there as it so often was, but he didn't turn around. He couldn't. If he saw her face he would lose what little resolve he had left.

He ripped the gown off from his chest, tossing it into the biohazard bin and ran his hands under the faucet, waiting for the water to come on. When it did, he began scrubbing his hands. He cursed out loud, slamming his hands onto either side of the stainless steel wash basin.

The patient had been a mother. She had two teenage daughters he'd met earlier that evening. It was a simple surgery, a routine appendectomy. He hadn't been counting on the unexpected mass in her cecum. They hadn't seen it in her scans. The tissue was inflamed and needed a resection in order to prevent an impending small bowel obstruction. The hemorrhage wasn't his fault. If he'd known about the issue beforehand, he could've had time to prepare a plan.

But, she was gone. And his hands had been the ones meant to save her. He scrubbed harder, until his fingers were red, raw, and nearly bleeding. A small tear fell from his eyes and he wiped it away with his arm just as the door opened again.

The patient had been closed up. The surgery was over. As the nurses began filing out, each avoiding his eye contact, he stared into the operating room, looking at the blood that still coated the floor, the blue sheet that now covered her face. Quinn left the room last, touching his arm. When he looked at her, her eyes were grim.

"You didn't know," she said.

It didn't matter. "I should have."

"You couldn't have. Her family didn't know. Her doctor didn't know. It's not your fault."

He pulled away from her grasp. "I have to go tell her family. They'll be waiting for news."

She was calm as ever, closing her eyes and taking a breath. She spoke in a low, throaty tone. "Take a moment, Jess," she warned. "Pull yourself together first."

He shook off his hands over the sink, running his palms down his face and taking a deep breath. She patted his shoulder as she walked past him. He nodded toward her, thankful for her words. She smiled sadly, her eyes kind.

The conversation that was coming was the worst part of his job. He'd take draining a thousand pus-filled lesions over just the one conversation. The one where he had to tell her family that his hands had been the only thing between her and death, and no matter how hard he had tried—he couldn't save her.

Lately, that seemed to be a pattern for him. Losing people, both patients and fiancées. He walked down the hall, trying to clear his head and drain the emotion from his body. He couldn't allow himself to feel when he spoke to them. He had to be empty.

He passed through the double doors, entering the waiting room, his scrub cap in hand. Her husband saw him immediately, his worried eyes growing wide as he stood. He read the look on Jesse's face before he spoke.

"No," he said, shaking his head as his face began to scrunch up. His sobs tore through the quiet, too-cold room. "No," he repeated. Beside him, the girls stood up, their smiling faces fading. They fell into each other's arms before Jesse could speak the first word.

"I'm so sorry," he told them, though they were no longer looking his direction. The husband, a husky fellow with a balding head sank into a chair, his body shaking. "Evelyn didn't make it through surgery." He spoke over their sobs, needing to say it out loud. "When we began, I ran into a problem. Your wife had a mass in her abdomen, which was causing a slight blockage of her lower intestine. She needed a resection, but she started to hemorrhage. We gave her two pints of blood, but her blood pressure kept dropping. Her heart was having to work too hard. My team and I did all that we could to save her, but I'm afraid we weren't able to." He paused, fiddling with the calluses on his palms. "Your wife is dead, Mr. Ramirez." He closed his eyes, taking a breath. It was required that they use the word: dead. Not *passed away*, not *gone on*, not *no longer with us*. It was imperative that the family understood completely, though the word always felt harsh when spoken.

He stood for a few moments, watching them cry, before the eldest daughter looked up to him. "Can we, um," she paused, wiping her eyes with shaking hands, "can we see her?"

He nodded. "Yes, of course. They're getting her ready for you now. In just a few moments, a nurse will be able to take you back."

"I don't understand," the husband said, "it was just a simple surgery. The other doctor told us there was nothing to worry about."

"Dr. Sloane never should have told you that. I'm sorry he did. With surgery, there is always risk." His response was automatic—programmed in him like a script.

"You said a mass...what is that? Like a tumor? Why didn't they find that before the surgery? How long had it been there?"

"It's possible that it was a tumor, though that doesn't mean it was cancer. It could certainly have been benign, but without a biopsy, I can't say for sure. As for why we didn't know about the mass, it's difficult to say why it didn't show up on her scans, but it was likely causing her no symptoms quite yet."

The man nodded, blinking his eyes through heavy tears.

"Would you like me to give you a moment?"

Again, the man nodded, leaning onto his daughter's shoulder. Jesse took a step back, relief filling him. He turned around, heading out of the waiting room. He didn't belong there anymore. As he passed through the double doors again, he felt a weight leave his chest, his breath filling his lungs completely again. It was over. He'd done his part. Soon, one of the nurses would be along to check on them. Maybe Quinn. She was good at that—consoling the broken. He knew because she'd done it so often with him.

"ARE you planning to come over tonight?" Quinn asked as they walked out of the locker room.

"Nah, I think I'll just head home."

"What? You're breaking tradition on me?"

"Yeah." He shrugged. "I just want to catch up on some sleep."

"Okay," she said, her eyes dancing between his, her brow low. "But...you're okay, right?"

"I'm fine, Q," he assured her, bowing his head. "I just need...I don't know...I just need a minute." They passed through the entrance to the hospital and out into the parking lot.

"Okay," she said, giving in, "but just don't go off and sulk alone. If you need something you'd better call me."

"I will."

She turned to walk away, jingling her keys over her head. "I'll see you tomorrow, right?"

"Tomorrow?" he asked, but the realization hit him as soon as he spoke. He opened his mouth again but no words came out. *Tomorrow. Reagan's wedding.*

"Are you sure you're—"

"Yeah, yep. Sorry, I just lost track of the day. I'll be there."

"You're picking me up, right?"

He nodded. "I'll be there around noon."

She smiled. "See you then."

He turned away from her, walking the opposite direction to his car. The fact that his ex-fiancée's wedding was tomorrow made his already miserable night one million times worse.

As he climbed into his car and pulled out of the parking lot, he headed right, rather than left. He wasn't going home, not alone and not tonight.

TWO

JESSE

Jesse sat at the long bar in the dark club, both hands wrapped around the crystal tumbler in front of him. He lowered his head, rolling his eyes as the beat grew louder from the speakers behind him. He wasn't sure why he had come; obnoxiously loud bars were definitely not his thing.

"Need another?" a voice called over the music. He looked up, surprised to see a new bartender behind the counter. She was dressed in a black and white polka dot tank top with skin tight red pants to match the lipstick on her full lips. She looked like a real-life pin-up girl, a headband stuck through her cola colored hair.

She blinked at him from behind long lashes. "Do you need another drink?" she asked again.

"Oh," he said, brought back to reality. He looked down into his glass, swirling the dark liquid around before picking it up and drinking the last of it. "I shouldn't," he told her honestly. He rarely drank anyway. In fact, it was rare he *could* drink with always being on call—the perks of being a surgical resident. But tonight was an exception. Because of her. Because he'd stupidly promised he'd come to the wedding. Because he always had to be the good guy. Anger and bourbon bubbled in his belly.

"Wife wouldn't want you to?" the woman asked, eyeing him as she took his glass away.

"No wife," he said, perhaps a bit of bitterness in his voice, wiggling his fingers so she could see they bore no ring.

"Girlfriend, then?" She spun around, putting the tumbler in a gray tub on the back counter.

"No girlfriend either."

She smirked at him. "What? A handsome guy like you?" She was patronizing him and he knew it. She leaned across the bar so he had a perfect view of her breasts. "Sounds like you *do* need another drink then."

He nodded, not really agreeing, but when she slid a new one to him he didn't bother arguing. He picked the glass up, his eyes locked with hers as he took a large gulp. "I'm Jesse," he told her when he set the glass back down.

"Novalee. But you can call me Nova."

He smirked. "Nova, huh? Like...supernova?"

"I used to think so." Her eyes showed a hint of sadness behind the heavy liner.

"What changed?" He finished off the glass, welcoming the burn.

"I grew up." She shrugged. "And, when I did, I realized there's nothing super about me at all."

He reached across the bar, instinctively reaching for a piece of her hair. She seemed surprised by his actions but didn't stop him. He twirled the hair around his finger carefully.

"I think you're pretty super." He laughed as the corny joke fell from his liquor-coated mouth. "Pretty pretty. Super pretty." He stopped, composing himself and started over. "I think you're pretty."

"I think I pour a *pretty* strong drink." She rolled her eyes at him, though her tone was light. "You're cut off after that one."

He furrowed his brow. "What? A man has to be drunk to think you're pretty?"

"No," she argued, a glimmer in her eyes. "I *am* pretty. But it takes a pretty strong drink for someone your age to have the guts to say it."

"My age? What's that—"

A man fell into him, interrupting their conversation. "Woah, sorry," he said, though he wasn't looking at Jesse. His eyes remained locked on the short blonde hanging onto his waist. "Two more beers, Nova," he demanded, laying a bill onto the counter. The girl, her cheetah print dress clinging to her curves, smiled at Jesse when she noticed him staring. Nova slid two beers across the counter and pulled the cash to her.

"There you go, Travis."

He took them without another word, turning around and heading for the opposite side of the room. Nova took the empty glass from Jesse without consent. He huffed. It *was* empty, and she was right about him not needing another, but that didn't give her the right to take it away. He was a paying customer just like the rest of them.

Before he could say anything, he noticed the sour look on her face. "You okay?" he asked.

She ran her tongue over her teeth, obviously agitated. "That was my ex-husband." She threw her hand over her shoulder in his direction. "A complete ass. He just..." She rubbed her temple, shaking her head. "Doesn't matter. You ready for your bill?" she asked, changing the subject quickly.

"Yeah, that's fine," he agreed. "Are you sure you're okay?"

"I'll be fine." Her smile was vulnerable, but her voice was far from it. She was tough. Unbreakable. Or perhaps she'd already been broken beyond repair. She tore a slip of white paper from the register and handed it to him. "You don't come in here very often, do you?"

He shook his head. "I don't spend much time in bars, to be honest."

"I didn't figure so. You don't look like the type."

He frowned. "There's a type?"

She pointed across the room to where her ex stood, his messy hair down to his shoulders and an untucked, unbuttoned flannel shirt hanging over his thin chest. "He's the type. You look like a city boy. A lawyer or something. Most of the folks we get around here look just like Travis."

"Actually, that's where you're wrong. I'm not a

lawyer." He didn't bother mentioning that he was a surgeon, which she might say was pretty close. "And I'm not a city boy, either. I'm from Dale," he said. "It's a few towns away, and I'm sure you've never heard of it because it's far from anything like a city."

She laughed, her hand covering her mouth.

"What? It's true," he insisted.

"Of course it is," she said, her laughter continuing.

"What is that supposed to mean?"

She shook her head, her laughter subsiding, and held her hands up in surrender. "Nothing. It's just...I know Dale. Pretty well actually. And that about sums up my night."

"No one knows Dale." He cocked his head to the side, trying to figure out if she was kidding.

"You're right about that. No one that isn't from there." She shook her head, pursing her lips.

"You're saying you're from Dale? Dale, Georgia? No way. I would've noticed you." He was shameless as he looked her up and down.

"You didn't hear me, honey. I'm old enough to be your mother. You wouldn't have had the chance. I probably left Dale before you were even born."

"Yeah, right," he said, feeling offended. "You're how old? Thirty-five?"

"Try adding ten years...and then some." She raised her eyebrows, folding her arms across her chest so her breasts pushed out even further.

He was shocked. She *was* his parents' age, but *damn*, no parents he knew looked like her.

"Yeah," she said pointedly, "not quite as hot now, am I?"

"Actually, I wasn't thinking that at all." And he wasn't.

"Good to know," she said simply, sliding his card back to him.

"So, what time do you get off?" he asked.

"Are you asking me out?" She sounded doubtful.

"Are you turning me down?" he challenged her.

"I don't date kids."

He let out a breath. "I can assure you, I'm no kid, Nova." He leaned over the bar, lowering his voice. "Come out with me and I'll be happy to prove it." The liquor was making him brave. It wasn't a line he would've used any other time. Nova was intriguing though—her eyes held both a mystery and immense pain, one begging to be solved, the other healed.

"You talk a big game." She batted her eyelashes. "But you should know I'm not interested in any sort of relationship."

"I'm not—"

"I'm just letting you know up front. I don't want it. I'm a recently divorced, happily single woman who's enjoying..." She pressed her lips into a small smile, like she had a secret. "Trying out new things."

"I don't want a relationship either," he assured her. "I was supposed to get married in a month. But that girl is marrying someone else tomorrow."

She didn't look apologetic. Instead she shrugged. "See, people suck."

"I couldn't agree more."

"So, me and you...it's just one night?"

"One night," he said firmly. "And we'll never have to see each other again."

"No falling in love, no strings."

"You don't even have to tell me your last name."

She frowned, grabbing a towel from behind her and wiping down the bar. "Let me get one of the girls to cover. I'll meet you in the parking lot in ten minutes."

"You can just leave like that?"

"Honey, I own the bar. I can do whatever the hell I want."

His head leaned to the side, surprised.

"What?" She laughed at his expression. "You didn't think you were talking to some poor damsel in distress, did you? I'm a powerful, middle-aged woman. You still wanna take me home or not?"

He placed his hand on the bar. "More than ever."

THREE

QUINN

Quinn made a U-turn. Her eleventh of the night. *Where the hell could he be?* He wasn't at home, he wasn't at her house. She was growing more worried by the minute.

Losing a patient was always bad, but this one Jesse had taken especially hard. She wanted to comfort him, but she could see it wasn't what he needed. He needed space and that was okay. But, that didn't mean she wasn't going to make sure he made it home safe.

She'd checked the only bar in Dale, and his car wasn't there. Could he have gone to see Reagan? Surely he wasn't *that* upset. It was so rare that she saw Jesse break composure, she wasn't honestly ever sure what to expect when he did. She drove past his house again, still no lights.

Headlights turned down the street, filling the darkness around her with light. She let out a sigh of relief when she saw it was his car. If he recognized hers, he was sure to give her crap about being a stalker when he saw her tomorrow. But it was worth it. At least she could relax knowing he was safe.

She turned back around one last time, a sudden vision of him spending the night passed out on the lawn in her head. It wasn't like him to drive drunk, in fact he was a stickler about how many drinks he'd allow himself, so she was sure it wouldn't be the case but she needed peace of mind.

She drove past slowly, watching him climb out of the car. He was sober, or at least not stumbling as he walked around to the passenger's door and let his date out.

She rolled her eyes, trying to see the woman in the dark driveway. She couldn't make her out. *Oh well,* she mused. He was safe, and that was what mattered. She tried to pretend the sting of jealousy wasn't overwhelming her as she drove out of sight unnoticed.

FOUR

JESSE

When they arrived at his house, Nova hadn't stopped smiling since they hit the town line. He stopped the car and hoped she didn't notice the nervous way his legs were shaking. Something like this was nearly unheard of for him. He was a relationship guy, but Reagan had changed all of that.

"You really are from Dale," she said.

"I told you."

"I haven't seen this town in years." Her voice was thoughtful as she stared out the window.

"I'm sure not much has changed."

"No," she said simply. "Nope. Not much."

He opened his door, stepping out of the car and walking around to her side. She opened her door. "This isn't a date, Jesse, you don't have to open my door for me."

"It's just a habit, sorry."

"Don't apologize, either."

"You certainly are demanding," he said, only half-joking.

She shrugged, walking past him when he opened the door to his house. "I know what I like."

He shut the door behind them. "And what's that?"

"I like men who don't ask too many questions." She set her purse down on the couch. "You have a nice place."

"Thank you," he said.

"It's a little big for just you." She nodded to the fireplace. "Is she yours?"

He turned around, glancing at the picture of him and Nora at the zoo last year. "No. Not really. She's my ex-fiancée's daughter."

"You kept the picture up?"

He bit his lip. "I didn't break up with her. I broke up with her mother. Or, she broke up with me." Why would he admit that? He wanted to smack himself in the face.

"You're a good guy, Jesse."

He nodded stiffly. "Not always, but I try to be."

"So, what's a good guy like you doing picking up random girls in a bar?"

"I don't know," he said, "you weren't exactly in my plan."

"Sure I was." Her eyes were warm, mysterious, as if she knew something he didn't.

He lowered his brow at her.

"Well, maybe not me, per say, but someone was in the plan tonight. I've worked that bar long enough to know when a man comes into a bar looking for something sweet to take home. You needed me."

His jaw tensed. "It wasn't like that."

"You had a bad day, Jess. You need a little...*release.*" Coming off her tongue, the word was like candy. He watched her perfect lips turn into a smile. "It's not a crime."

"I don't want you to think I do this all the time. I'm not some...I'm not someone who does this."

"Oh, no, I thought you were an old pro at this. You're doing it so well," she said with a wink. "Relax, baby. We're just having some fun." She took a step toward him, running a finger down the buttons on his shirt. His breath caught in his chest, his heart pounding.

"I'm just...it's been a while since I've been with anyone new. My ex and I—"

She held up a finger, cutting him off. "We aren't friends, Jesse. This is just a physical thing. You don't owe me any sort of explanation."

He touched her chin, pulling her face up to his. "Okay, then. How about no talking at all?"

She seemed relieved. "That's perfect." She stood up, pressing her lips to his. She tasted like spearmint gum. His tongue pushed its way into her mouth and her hands gripped his back. She moved her mouth to his neck, biting it playfully, and he let out a breath.

She stepped back. "Which way is the bedroom?" she asked.

He pointed down the hall, beginning to head that direction, but she stopped him. "Then we want to go anywhere but there." She walked to the kitchen, climbing up onto the table and swinging her legs back and forth. "Too intimate for my taste."

He nodded, walking to her and grabbing ahold of her hair, pulling her head back. He licked her neck, his teeth grazing her skin as she moaned. He reached down, pulling off her shirt so he could get a better look at her. She pulled the straps of her bra off her shoulders carefully, finally reaching back and undoing her bra so her breasts bounced free. He cupped them, running his thumbs over her nipples. Her head fell back, eyes rolling in ecstasy.

Her hands went to his belt, untucking his shirt with haste. He reached up to help her, unbuttoning each button as fast as his fingers could move. He smiled at her wickedly, only realizing then how right she had been. He did need release. He needed to escape. And she was proving to be the perfect hideaway.

FIVE

JESSE

They laid on the kitchen floor, their breathing wild and unrelenting. He looked over at her, running a finger through the mess of hair on the floor. She sat up, pulling the hair away from him quickly and looked down.

"Uh-oh," she said, staring between his legs.

He looked down, to where the condom lay, its end split in two. "Shit," he cursed, "oh *shit.*" He sat up, his pulse racing. He grabbed part of the condom off the floor, pulling the rest off of him. There was no telling how old the thing was. "What do we do?"

She grabbed her pants from the back of the chair. "I take it this has never happened to you before?"

He shook his head. "It has for you?"

"Not too often." She pulled her shirt over her head. "What can I say? I like it a little rough."

"What do we do?" he asked again.

"I'll take a morning after pill, no big deal. I'm old, remember? My eggs are all shriveling up anyway."

He reached for his shirt across from him, pulling it on and grabbing for his boxers. "You aren't old."

"Relax darlin', you already got what you wanted. You don't have to sweet talk me now."

"It's not like that," he argued, approaching her as she pulled her pants over her hips.

She touched his chest, preventing him from approaching her. "Jesse, you don't have to—"

He took hold of her hand. "I'm not doing you any favors. I'm telling you the truth. *You aren't old.* And I had a lot of fun with you tonight. If you don't want to see me again, that's fine, but don't act like that's on me. *I had fun with you,*" he repeated, "you're sexy as hell." He grabbed her back, pulling her close to him. "And I'd be more than happy to prove it. Again." He was growing hard against her leg, his body ready for round two. He leaned down, his lips headed for hers but she turned away, his mouth landing on her cheek. She took a step back.

"I told you. I told you I didn't want anything other than tonight. I told you this was only meant to be physical." She seemed mad.

He backed away from her, suddenly feeling defensive. "And it can be."

"Apparently not," she snapped.

"You're being ridiculous. I'm just trying to be nice to you."

"Exactly. And I don't need that. What I needed was a

night to get my mind off of my *shit*-life and I thought that was what you needed, too."

"It was," he insisted, pulling his pants on in a hurry. "Nothing has to happen. I was only suggesting—"

She stormed away from him, rushing into the living room and grabbing her purse. "I have to go."

"Wait, Nova, where are you going to go? You don't have a car. Let me at least take you home."

"I have some family I plan to visit while I'm here in town. I can get myself there." She wasn't looking his way as she walked out of the house and into the darkness of the night. He wanted to call after her, demand that she wait, but in the end he stood still watching her disappear before his eyes.

SIX

JESSE

Jesse stood outside of Quinn's door, waiting. He looked at his phone, checking the time before knocking again. Finally, he pulled out his key, sticking it into the lock and yelling into the house. "Q? You here? We're going to be late if we don't get going."

He stepped into the house, shutting the door. After a moment, he heard her heels heading down the hall upstairs. "Yeah, yeah, hold your horses."

He smiled as he heard her sarcastic tone. When she came around the corner, descending the stairs, he took a breath. She was poking her last earring through her ears. Once it was in place, she looked up at him and smiled casually, completely unaware of how beautiful she looked.

The simple red dress hugged her hips, her auburn hair had been pinned back. She wore a diamond pin just above her left ear, a small tendril of hair already escaping it.

"Woah," he said softly, not realizing the word had escaped his mouth until she laughed.

"What?" she asked. "You think you're the only one around here who can clean up?" She flicked his shoulder.

He swallowed, pulling his eyes away from her dress. "No, I've just...never seen you so dressed up." He grabbed her white coat from the hook, holding it out for her to slide her arms in.

"I can't exactly wear scrubs to her wedding, Jess." She pulled open the door, oblivious to his dangerous, friendship-altering thoughts. "Let's go."

Following her lead, he walked out the door and waited for her to lock it. They walked down the faded sidewalk to where his car was waiting. He opened her door, allowing her to climb in.

"Someone's feeling chivalrous," she said, tucking her chin into her shoulder shyly.

"Don't get used to it," he teased, walking around to his side. He started the car.

"So, how are we going to handle this?" she asked as they headed out of town.

"Huh?"

"Copious amounts of alcohol? A last minute profession of your love minutes before they say 'I do'? Want me to take Gunner around back and..." She made a clicking noise with her tongue, wiggling her shoulders. "Give him a distraction?"

He rolled his eyes. "No. We're going to let them be."

Her eyes were serious. "All joking aside, Jess, are you going to be okay? I still think you're a saint for even considering going to her wedding."

"I'll be fine," he said. "She's happy. That's what matters."

"You're too good of a guy for her. She doesn't deserve you."

"Watch it," he warned. Quinn had always had an attitude about Reagan, but since their breakup things had gotten worse.

She placed her hands in her lap. "I just...I wish she saw how much better you are than Gunner James. Because you are."

"And you aren't the least bit biased," he joked, reaching over and squeezing her hand. "Let's not worry about it. I'm just glad you could be here with me. I couldn't do this without you."

"Always," she promised. "What are best friends for?"

WHEN THEY ARRIVED at the church in Atlanta, they were both exhausted. Quinn walked ahead of him, limping dramatically as she rubbed the back of her thighs.

"Man, your car is so uncomfortable."

"Sorry, your highness. It was a three-hour ride on leather seats, what did you expect?"

She snorted, winking. "Well, I've never had a three-hour ride before and I'm more of a latex girl."

"Are you twelve?" He scowled, though he couldn't

hide the smirk that grew on his face. Nerves were beginning to fill his stomach as they walked into the church, her arm wrapped through his. They made their way to a pew in the back, trying to remain out of sight. He was worried they were going to be late, but the ceremony still hadn't begun.

Quinn looked his way, her eyes full of worry, but she remained silent.

"I swear I'm fine," he told her under his breath.

"Her parents are staring at you."

He looked up, making eye contact with the Orricks and offering them a small smile. He sighed when they looked away. "Let's just get this over with."

"Think anyone would notice if we just disappeared out the back?" she teased him. "'Cause I'm totally down for that."

He stared at her, so grateful she was there with him. He was so tempted to reach up and move the piece of hair that was coming close to her eyes. She shook her head at his stares, unaware of how completely beautiful he couldn't help but find her in that moment. How had he missed it before? It wasn't just the makeup, he'd seen Quinn dressed up plenty of times, something was different tonight. Something about her smile was warming the parts of his heart that he had thought would remain cold forever. What in the world was happening to him? That was Quinn he was thinking about. He was being ridiculous.

Before he could respond, the organ began playing and the entire room grew still as the back doors opened, making way for the wedding party. He watched Nora, Reagan's daughter, walk down the aisle. Her dark hair had been curled tightly, something he remembered her hating. She smiled at him and he gave her a thumbs up, his throat tight as he couldn't help but picture himself waiting at the end of the aisle, a place where he'd intended to be only a few short months ago. Before Gunner came back.

He felt Quinn's hand running down his arm, her fingers laced with his, reaffirming that he could make it through this god-awful day. He held onto hers when she moved to pull away. Just then, the doors were closed and the familiar wedding march began to play. The crowd stood up at once, welcoming the bride as she passed through the opening doors and headed down the aisle. She was every bit as beautiful as he'd imagined.

Quinn's thumb ran over his knuckles as Reagan passed. Her eyes met his for only a moment before they landed back at the end of the aisle, where they belonged. When she'd reached Gunner, the guests sat and Quinn let go of his hand. He nodded at her as they settled into the ceremony. *He was okay.* And the further into the wedding they grew, the more he realized how true that was. He'd loved Reagan. He'd loved the idea of building a life with her. That was all true, but the longer he sat, next to the woman who'd been his best friend for so long, the more he realized how okay he was. And how responsible for that Quinn was.

As he thought about Quinn, his mind drifted to Nova, the woman from the past night, who was so utterly alone and seemed to have no plans of changing that. What had a broken heart done to her? What had her ex turned her into?

Whatever it was, he was determined to make sure his ending was different. Reagan Orrick wouldn't be the end of his love story.

SEVEN

JESSE

Jesse shook Gunner's hand. "Take care of her," he said, trying to keep his voice light.

"I plan to." Gunner nodded.

"You look great," he told Reagan. "The wedding was beautiful. I'm happy for you both." She leaned forward, hugging him. Her familiar smell overwhelmed him and he pulled away.

"Thank you for coming, Jesse," she said with tears in her eye. "Really, thank you. You have no idea what it means to me."

"Yes, I do. And you're welcome." He looked down to Nora, rubbing her head. "You did great, Nor. Prettiest maid of honor I've ever seen."

"I have a real family now, Jesse," she squealed, her face beaming with excitement.

He kissed her forehead, a lump in his throat. "Yes,

kiddo, you sure do." Her arms went around his neck and she kissed his cheek. "I love you," he whispered in her ear.

"I love you too, Jesse," she said with a smile.

It was all he could take and Quinn seemed to sense that. After she offered her congratulations to the couple, she pushed him forward and down the church stairs without stopping. "Come on," she said, when they were out of earshot. "You deserve a drink."

"OKAY, okay, but seriously...what are you going to do now?" Quinn laughed over her drink.

"What do you mean what am I going to do now? We have work the day after tomorrow."

"I mean, like, with your life. You're free now...are you going to stay in Dale? Are you going to move to Chicago like you wanted to before you met Reagan?"

"I'm *free* now? What was I before? A prisoner?"

She pressed her lips together. "You know what I mean. I just...you have the world at your fingertips. You're this young, handsome surgeon...you can do anything you want."

"Handsome?" He wiggled his eyebrows at her.

"Oh, shut up. Moderately attractive is more like it. Not total garbage." She smiled widely, her whole face lighting up.

"Well, what about you? You could do anything you wanted, too."

She shook her head, taking another sip of her drink. "It's different for me."

"How?"

"It just is. Don't change the subject."

A waitress walked past, her eyes locked on Jesse. "Can I get you guys another round?"

"I think we're okay for now," Jesse told her.

She nodded, running her fingers along the table. "Let me know if that changes."

Quinn laughed when she was far enough away not to notice.

"What?" Jesse asked.

"You don't notice it."

"Notice what?"

"The effect you have on people," she mused.

"What effect?"

She sighed, rolling her eyes. "Oh, nevermind."

"You can't change the subject," he said, rolling the glass in his hands.

"What, like you aren't changing the subject about Chicago?" Her eyes narrowed at him.

He set the glass down, staring at his fingers. "I don't know if I'll go to Chicago."

"Do you still have the offer for the hospital up there once you finish your residency?"

He nodded. "I do." She bit her lip. "But I don't know if I'll take it. Honestly, I haven't made up my mind."

She took another drink, her eyes studying him. "I thought Chicago was what you wanted? Reagan was the one who didn't want to leave Dale."

"That's true. But, it's not necessarily what I want now. A lot has changed in the past year."

"Like what?"

"Like, I'm not planning to sell the house anymore. Work is going well. I'm happy where I am. Maybe I'll go to Chicago. Hell, maybe I'll go to Seattle. But maybe I'll stay where I am and see how things go." He watched a small smile grow on her face and couldn't help but smile himself. "That makes you happy?"

She laughed it off, reaching back and letting her hair out of its clips. It fell down beside her face casually, still wavy from being pinned. "Of course it makes me happy, you big doof. You're my best friend. Do you know how boring my life would be without you?"

He nodded. "Yep. I am the most entertaining person you know, without a doubt."

She finished off the last of her drink, holding her hand in the air for the waitress. "What happened to you last night, by the way?"

"Oh, I just went home." He wasn't sure why he was lying, but something in him didn't want Quinn to know about Nova. On a normal day, he would've already spilled his guts about her...letting Quinn dissect the night. But, this was no normal day.

"Mhm," she said, looking skeptical.

"What?"

"Since when do you ever go home after you lose a patient? You always come over. It's routine. It's like...a ceremony at this point."

"Pizza and beer is our losing-a-patient ceremony?" His smile grew so big it hurt his cheeks.

"Or anything else sad. My parents splitting up, Reagan losing her mind...you know, the usual."

"God, we're lame."

"I like our tradition," she said, pushing out her bottom lip in a fake pout.

"I like our tradition, too," he said, his voice low. The waitress approached, bringing them each a new drink. She smiled at Jesse, barely looking Quinn's way.

"Thank you," Quinn said loudly, dismissing her. When she was gone, she looked back at Jesse. "I'm proud of you."

"You are?" He cocked his head to the side in confusion.

"The way you handled today. And the way you handle that little girl. It's sweet."

"Nora's a good kid," he said, uncomfortable with her compliment.

"You have a soft spot for her." She began picking at the skin around her pinky nail. "Right before my dad left...god, it was like I was the only bargaining chip left in their relationship. They'd put me in the middle of every fight. I was the pawn. But you and Reagan, it's like you both just love her so much."

"It's not the same, Q," he said softly, "she's not mine to love. Or bargain with for that matter."

"I know, it's just..."

"She's with her parents now. I was never her dad. I

want what's best for her, and I know this is it. No matter how bad it stung at first."

"That's exactly my point. You want what's best for everyone. Everyone except yourself. What you've done is noble, Jesse. Walking away like you did."

"What choice did I have?"

Her eyes locked with his, her cheeks flushing. "I'm not saying you made the wrong choice. The opposite, in fact. I'm saying you made the right choice, but now it's time for you to make a choice for yourself. You need something for yourself."

"Oh, yeah? And what do you suggest?"

"What do you want to do? More than anything? What would make you happy?"

He stared at her, his eyes traveling to her red lips and then back up to her eyes. "I don't...I don't know," he fumbled the words as they came out, clearing his throat.

"You have to know," she insisted.

"Well, what would make you happy?"

"This isn't about me. You have to think about yourself, Jess. For once in your life."

"Are you honestly scolding me for being too...*selfless?*"

She laughed. "I'm being selfish for you."

"Where is this all coming from?"

She tucked a piece of hair behind her ear, trailing her hand down the neckline of her dress. His eyes followed her hand, his body heating up. "Today hurt my heart for you, that's all." Her voice was low. He leaned forward, trying to hear her better.

"You don't have to worry about me, Q. You know that."

"I do," she agreed. "But I worry anyway. I just want you to be happy, you know that, right?"

He took a large drink, needing some liquid courage to go along with the dangerous thoughts roaring through his mind. "Are you? Happy, I mean."

She nodded. "Tonight? Very." She scrunched up her nose playfully. "In life? I'm getting there."

"Are you still dating what's-his-face?"

"Who?"

"You know...fedora-boy." He made a skeptical face.

She laughed. "Daniel? God, no. That was months ago."

"He didn't make the cut, huh?"

She shook her head slowly, looking down and running a finger over the rim of her glass. "He didn't...make the cut."

"Well, that's a shame."

"Is it?" She made a face that showed she knew he wasn't mourning the loss too much.

"Do you want me to lie?"

"Don't you want me to be happy?"

"Did fedora-boy make you happy?"

"What is this? Twenty questions?"

He winked. "Do you want it to be?"

"Can you keep it going?" She laughed loudly.

"Do you want me to go all night?" He lowered his voice so it came out in a growl that made her laugh harder.

"No, to answer your question, *Daniel,*" she stressed his name, "didn't make me happy."

"It was the fedora, wasn't it? Did he make you wear it? Did it smell? It looked like that thing had never been washed."

She slapped his arm, laughing hysterically. "Stop!" She held her stomach, her cheeks flushing. "The fedora wasn't the issue. He just...wasn't my type."

"Tall, dark, and handsome?"

"Nah," she teased, running a hand through his golden locks, "I prefer blonds."

"Well, too bad for you, because I don't own any fedoras. I know those were important to you."

She threw her head back, sighing loudly. "Jesse Mathis, what on earth am I going to do with you?"

"Fall in love with me, probably," the words slipped out of his mouth without conscious thought. Her head popped back up, her face ashen.

"What?"

He tried to recover. "Joke, woman. It was a joke."

She pretended to laugh, though the tension was glaringly obvious between them. It was a tension they'd never known before. Things were always easy with Quinn. He'd never had to worry about what he looked like or said. It wasn't like how he felt with other girls. But, something that night was different. Something in him had changed.

He blinked quickly, shaking his head to clear the thought. This was *Quinn* he was thinking about. Quinn his best friend. Quinn who he talked to about everything.

No way could anything ever happen between them. If this tension was bad, he couldn't imagine the tension if she didn't feel the same. Or worse, if she did and their relationship ended in a breakup.

No. He was just rebounding from Reagan, and there was no way in hell Quinn would be his rebound. She deserved better.

"Well," she said, pressing the home button on her phone to check the time, "it's getting late. I guess we had better get going."

"I'm in no shape to drive," he told her. "Are you?"

She thought for a minute. "No, not really. You wanna stay?"

He nodded. "There's a hotel up the street. We can grab a room for the night."

"Yeah, that's probably a good idea," she agreed, standing up.

"I'll go pay our tab. Wait here."

"Nope," she grabbed his arm. "This one's on me."

"What? No way. You aren't paying for my drinks."

"You always pay when we go out, J. This one was my treat to make up for your day. Let me take you out for once," she said, batting her eyelashes.

He sighed. "Are you sure?"

"Yep, I'm sure," she responded, grabbing her purse from the back of the chair. "But, fine, if you're going to twist my arm about it, I guess you can pay for the hotel room." She smiled at him slyly.

He chuckled. "Oh, well that seems fair."

"I knew you would think so," she said. "Wait here."

She headed to the bar and began chatting instantly with the bartender. Jesse looked him over, his long dark hair pulled into a low bun. Thick, black frame glasses sat on his nose. He was the kind of guy Quinn dated. He watched the two of them talking for several minutes before Quinn turned back around, a giant smile on her face.

"Did you pay for the drinks?" he asked when she made her way back to him.

"Nope," she exclaimed, "didn't have to."

"Meaning what?"

"Meaning you aren't the only one around here with an effect on people, Jesse Mathis."

Well, that seemed to be for sure.

EIGHT

JESSE

Jesse stared at himself in the hotel mirror as he stripped out of his suit. He laid the jacket across the sink, folding his shirt carefully on top of it. He was pulling his pants off when he heard a knock on the room's door. He froze, pulling his pants back up and walking out of the bathroom.

"Thank you," Quinn was saying to someone outside of the door. She had changed into a fluffy white robe. She shut the door and turned back to face him. "I called down and had them bring us up some things." She held out a tube of toothpaste, two toothbrushes, and a comb.

He took a toothbrush from her hand. "Good idea," he said, looking her up and down. "Where'd you get the robe?"

"It was in the closet. There's one for you too."

He walked to the closet, pulling a robe off the large hanger. "Are you sure these are clean?"

"They're white so they can bleach them. They're about as clean as that comforter, I'm sure. Besides, what choice do we have? We didn't pack anything." She shrugged.

"True," he said, pulling the robe off his shoulders and removing his pants carefully. She averted her eyes, her face growing red. "What?" he asked. "It's not like you haven't seen it all before."

She turned away. "Oh, I know," she said lightly, "but that doesn't mean I *want* to see it again."

He scoffed. "You look at naked asses all day in the pit. I promise you mine looks better than most."

"Well, someone's cocky, aren't they?" She walked over and sat on one of the beds, grabbing the remote.

"Anything good on?" he asked, heading to the bathroom to brush his teeth. He heard her flipping through the channels and then after a moment, she joined him, running her toothbrush under the water.

They brushed in silence for a few moments, their eyes staring at each other in the mirror. It wasn't like they hadn't stayed together overnight before. Jesse stayed at Quinn's house more often than his own, especially lately. But being somewhere new, feeling what he was feeling, made it all seem different. She was different. He was different. Tonight, their relationship was just...*different.* He couldn't explain it. He spit into the sink, rinsing his brush. She pushed past him, doing the same.

"So, you ever going to tell me what you really did last night?" she asked.

"I went to a bar," he answered.

"Alone?"

"Yeah." He walked past her and out of the bathroom.

"Why didn't you invite me?"

"I just needed to be alone," he said carefully. "I took that patient's death really hard." He sat on the bed with one knee bent up under him.

"I know," she said, sitting in front of him. "I know you did. That's why I was so worried. I wanted to help you cope."

"You couldn't have helped me through that." He rubbed his forehead. "Trust me, there was nothing anyone could've done. It was just a bad night."

"I know. I lost her too, you know. Just because I'm not the surgeon doesn't mean I feel the loss any less." As if to prove her point, her voice cracked as she spoke.

"I know that, Q. I do. It's just..."

"Your heart is broken," she said matter-of-factly.

"What? No," he said, his voice full of denial.

"Jess, your heart is broken. And that's okay. It's normal. But, it makes everything else that goes wrong in your life seem so much more immense. Trust me, I get it. The point of this conversation is that you don't have to suffer alone. I'm here if you need to talk. Or vent. Or drink. However you want to cope, I can be there like I always have been. I'm not used to you shutting me out."

"I don't mean to shut you out. It's just that I know how you felt about Reagan."

"What? That she's not good enough for you?"

"Yeah, that," he said with a smile.

"Jess, I would never let how I feel about her affect how I support you. I never thought she was good enough for you, but you could've bet I would've been front row at that wedding. If you need to talk about losing her, then talk. I'm here. I can catch you."

"What if you don't know I'm falling?"

"I'll always know," she told him carefully. "It's what I do."

"How do you know so much about broken hearts? I've never seen you make it as far as the fifth date with a guy."

"Doesn't mean I don't know anything about love," she said. "In fact, it makes me an expert at broken hearts."

"How's that? Did fedora-boy hurt you?" He felt anger growing in him.

She grinned, placing a hand on his chest. "Nah, I hurt myself."

"What are you talking about?" His chest was growing tight as her hand rested half on his robe and half on his bare skin. He was sure she must feel his heart pounding.

She pulled her hand away. "Nothing. I just...I don't ever let anyone get close enough to hurt me. And, somehow, I guess that hurts me anyway."

He leaned forward, rubbing his thumb along the side of her face. "Any guy stupid enough to hurt you doesn't deserve you."

Her breathing hitched as she stared at him, her eyes remaining open and afraid. He could feel her breath on his skin. "My point exactly," she whispered, finally breaking eye contact.

"Your point?" He pulled his hand away.

"If Reagan was stupid enough to hurt you...you deserve someone who will love you the right way."

"Someone like who?" he asked her, begging her to look back at him as she picked at a loose thread on the comforter.

She frowned, standing up suddenly and making her way to her own bed. "I'm sure that waitress would be happy to take a shot." She ended the conversation with a snarky response, one that deflated the air from his chest instantly. She pulled the covers back, untying her robe and sliding out of it. "Look away," she told him, though she didn't look to see if he'd listened as she climbed into bed in only her bra and panties.

"You okay?" he asked her once she was covered. She held onto the remote tight, flipping off her lamp.

"I'm fine. Why?" She didn't bother looking up.

He walked over, climbing into her bed, though he stayed on top of the covers. "You seem sad. Are you in love with Gunner?" he joked.

She pulled away, raising her eyebrows. "Are you on crack?" she asked loudly.

"It wouldn't be the craziest thing. You've been off since the wedding."

"I've been off a lot longer than that," she said with a scoff. "Maybe it just took the wedding for you to notice."

"What are you talking about?" he asked. She laid her head over on his chest.

"It's not important, Jesse, it really isn't. It's late and I've had too much to drink. We should just go to sleep."

He leaned his head over onto hers. "Do you mind if I stay here?"

"I never do."

He kissed the top of her head, breathing in her scent. "Goodnight, Q."

"Goodnight," she told him, letting out a long sigh. He squeezed her arm, letting her warmth fill him more than the hot air from the vent directly above his head.

NINE

JESSE

"Will you go with me to the botanical gardens tonight?" Quinn asked him, handing over a patient's chart.

"What for?" he asked, eyeing the chart.

"Because I have two passes. I won them a while back, and I've been saving them for Christmas."

"They're the same lights every year," he said, only half listening.

She sighed, turning to walk away. "Fine, I'll go on my own."

He grabbed her arm. "No, stop. I'll take you."

"I don't need you to *take me,* you dork. I'm not four-teen. I just thought you could use something to do and I have a spare ticket. We had fun last year. But if you don't want to, don't worry about it."

"Mathis, Carter needs you in OR one," a stern voice

bellowed from behind them. Jesse spun around to face Janise, the chief resident.

"On my way," he said, beginning to walk off. He turned back to face Quinn one last time, as she had already begun talking to another nurse. "We'll go. I'll talk to you later," he called to her.

He walked down the hall through two sets of double doors and into the scrub room. He pulled his scrub cap on, reaching for a mask and pulling it over his ears. As he grabbed a scrub brush package and opened it, he looked through the glass, trying to find a familiar face in the room. It wasn't his usual team. He began scrubbing his hands, letting the hot water scald him.

"Hey," Melody Carter said as she walked into the room.

"Hey, what's going on?" he asked, looking into the next room at the patient on the table.

"Patient has coronary atherosclerosis. We originally planned to go in for a balloon angioplasty with a stent, but we found too many blockages. You're going to do a bypass graft instead." She pulled her hair back, wrapping it carefully before placing her cap and face mask on.

"Wait, *I'm* going to?" He moved up, scrubbing his arms carefully.

She nodded. As he finished, she stepped up to begin washing her hands. He walked into the operating room, grabbing a sterile towel pack and patting his hands dry. He let a nurse help him into his gown.

"No offense," he said, holding his hands out as the

nurse slipped them on. "But why am I here? I'm general. I thought Jensak was your right-hand with cardio."

"Normally, she is." Carter entered the room behind him, her voice slightly muffled behind her mask.

"So, what changed?"

"You're asking the wrong doctor, Mathis. These orders came straight from the chief."

"The chief? Since when does he assign residents?"

She shrugged again. "Are you complaining? You're about to do surgery. If you don't want to help—"

"No, no," he said as the nurse turned on the operating light, "I want to help. Forget I said anything."

She nodded, approaching the table. "All right then. It's forgotten."

"CHIEF NORWOOD," Jesse called after the man as he made his way down the crowded hall.

"Doctor Mathis," Norwood said, not bothering to stop walking, "what can I do for you?"

"I, um," he cleared his throat, finally catching up to him. "I wanted to thank you for letting me scrub in on the cardio surgery with Doctor Carter this morning."

"Ah," he said, his voice calm, "surgery went well, then?"

"Very well. The patient's in recovery now."

"Excellent," the chief said, waving at a man in a suit as he passed. "Is there anything else I can do for you, son?"

"No, that was it." He paused, continuing to walk with him. "I, um, was there any reason you wanted me on that surgery? It's just...I'm usually on general. I decided against cardio during my internship."

"Oh," he said, stopping in his tracks, "I just assumed you knew. The patient was a friend of your father's. He asked me to have you scrubbed in as a personal favor. While I don't normally condone that sort of thing, it's always nice to have Big Jim owe you a favor."

Jesse smiled uneasily. He was used to the kind of influence his father had over the town of Dale, but usually it didn't interfere in his work. He wanted to become a surgeon that was requested based on his own skill, not his father's demands. "Right. Well, thank you again." He turned down the hallway on his left, anger filling him.

Quinn was exiting a patient's room. She stopped when she saw him, her jaw dropping. "What's wrong?" she asked intuitively.

"Nothing," he grunted, walking past her.

She hurried to catch up. "I heard Carter let you scrub in. Did something go wrong?"

"No," he said, "everything was fine. I just found out my father asked for me to be on that surgery because it was his friend."

"And?" she asked, not understanding. "Is that a bad thing?"

"I don't want to be on surgeries because of who my dad is. I want them because I've earned them."

"I'm sure the chief wouldn't have put you on the

surgery if he didn't think you deserved it, Jess. And every-thing went fine, so you proved yourself."

He shook his head, his hands in fists. "I know. It's just frustrating. When I heard Carter was requesting me...I thought—"

"You thought you were just that good?" she said, trying to lighten things up.

He stopped, looking at her and then looking down, his head hung. "Yeah. I did. It was stupid, I guess."

"It's not stupid to want to get noticed around here." She put her hand on his shoulder, leaning forward so her eyes were locked with his. "And you *are* doing a good job. Don't let your dad cloud that."

He nodded. "I've got to go, I'm due in the OR."

"Are we still on for tonight, then?"

"Tonight?" he asked, only half listening.

"Nevermind," she said simply, waving her hand.

"Okay," he told her, disappearing down the hall, already lost in thought.

TEN

JESSE

"How've you been?" his mother asked as she opened the door to greet him. It was as if she'd been expecting him, but then that was how it always seemed.

"Fine," he lied.

"How was the wedding?" she asked, holding her arms out for him. She was dressed in one of her famous pantsuits, pastel green this time. Her blonde hair hung down over her shoulders, brushing over his face as he hugged her.

"It was fine." He patted her back.

"The Orricks said that girl spent a fortune on it." She tutted. "Probably a fortune on that ridiculous church alone. Why on earth wasn't a church here in Dale good enough? We have such pretty ones. Your father just helped the Methodist church get new stained glass. They wouldn't have charged her a penny to use their building."

He shrugged, stepping in the door. "I guess that's not what she wanted."

"*That girl* doesn't know what she wants," she said under her breath.

He frowned, taking off his jacket and placing it on the arm of the couch, desperately wanting to change the subject. "Is Dad home?"

She glanced at the clock on the wall. "He should be home any minute. Are you going to stay for dinner? I've got pork chops ready. There's plenty."

"Sure," he agreed.

"Great," she said, a bright smile on her red lips. "I'm going to run and change. Would you mind watching the potatoes for me? They're just about done."

"Okay." He walked into the kitchen, approaching the stove. He grabbed the sour cream from the counter, throwing in an extra scoop before anyone could catch him. He stirred the pot quickly, placing the spoon down when he heard the front door open.

Big Jim's heavy footsteps could be heard throughout the house as he made his way into the kitchen. He opened the refrigerator in search of a soda.

"Hey, Dad," Jesse greeted him.

His father lifted his head up, looking around. His eyes landed on Jesse, a smile spreading to his face. "Jess? What on earth are you doing here?"

"I came for supper," he said, grabbing three plates from the cabinet and walking to set them out on the table.

"Well, it's good to see you." Big Jim patted his shoulder as he walked past. "It's been a little while."

"Yeah, things have been busy," Jesse said.

"I hear you're doing great at work."

"From who?" Jesse asked, a bit too much of an attitude in his voice.

"What?"

"Who did you hear that from?"

"What do you mean? Just around town."

"I was called into a surgery today. A surgery that you apparently set me up for. Why would you do that?"

"Why would I ask you to do your job?" Big Jim seemed genuinely confused.

"You know I don't like you meddling in my work."

"Excuse me? *Meddling?* What are you talking about, Jess? When have I ever *meddled* in anything you do? I had a dear friend who was having surgery. I told him I could pull a few strings and get the best surgeon I knew on his case." He touched his shoulder again, holding his soda in his other hand. "I'm sorry if that upset you, son, I was trying to do something nice for him. And for you. I thought you'd be happy."

Jesse lowered his head, rubbing his brow. "I'm sorry. You're right." He sighed. "It's just been a long day."

"What's going on?" his father asked.

"It's just...it's nothing. Work has been crazy. I'm just tired, I guess."

His father nodded. "Do you need to go lie down? Your mother just washed the guest room sheets."

"No," Jesse said, "I'll probably head over to Quinn's for the—" he stopped. "Shit." He slapped a hand to his forehead. "I've got to go."

His mother walked into the room dressed in a t-shirt and jeans. "What's going on?"

"I'm not staying for supper," Jesse said in a panic. "I forgot I made plans. I have to go." He hurried into the living room, grabbing his coat from the couch and throwing it over his shoulders.

"What plans? What's the rush?" His mother's wild eyes searched his.

"It's okay." He kissed her cheek. "Everything's fine. I promised Quinn I'd meet her. I completely forgot." He glanced at his phone. "She's going to kill me."

ELEVEN

JESSE

Jesse wandered through the garden looking for her. The hot chocolate in his hands wasn't doing much to warm him in the bitter, December air. He checked his phone again, wondering if she'd returned his text, but the screen was blank. He turned down a path that seemed crowded, searching the groups of faces. She was nowhere to be found.

He zigzagged through, passing excited children and cozy couples. The museum at the top of the hill was his only chance to get warm, and so he decided he could search for her there.

He began trudging up the large, paved hill when suddenly he saw her. Her beige wool coat was wrapped around her, her auburn hair weighed down by an earwarmer wrapped around her head.

"Quinn!" he called to her, beginning to jog.

She turned around, her cheeks pink from the cold. "Jess?" she asked, unable to hide her apparent excitement. "I thought you weren't coming."

"I told you I'd be here, didn't I?"

She pursed her lips. "A half hour ago."

He nodded. "I know, I'm sorry. I had to go talk to my dad and I almost forgot."

"How did you get in?" She looked around. "I never gave you my other ticket."

He shook his head, raising an eyebrow. "You know they sell tickets at the gate, right?"

"You *paid* to come here? But you didn't think it was worth it, even for free." She trailed off, her eyes squinting as she tried to understand.

"It's not, but you are and I wasn't going to let you down. You asked me to be here, so here I am." He held out his arms to his sides as if he were a prize.

She wrapped an arm around him. "You're the best. Have I ever told you that?"

He chuckled. "Not lately." His arm went around her shoulder and he began to lead her toward the building. "Now, let's get inside before we freeze."

She took the hot chocolate from his hand without needing permission, taking a drink. "Ahh, that's amazing." She groaned. "So, how did it go with your dad?"

"I don't know. Fine, I guess."

"Fine means not good." She held open the door for him, but he stepped back, allowing her to walk in first.

"No, this time 'fine' really means fine. He said he didn't mean to do anything wrong. He claims he was just trying to help. I probably just overreacted, he gets under my skin so easily with his—ugh, it doesn't matter. It's fine, honestly. I guess it was just a friend who was worried about surgery."

"And he wanted you?" She looked skeptical.

"Hey, what's that supposed to mean?" he growled at her, pretending to be offended.

She put her arm back around his waist, syncing up their steps. "Nothing. I'm just kidding."

"Jesse?" a voice called from behind them.

Jesse turned around to see where the voice was coming from and stopped in his tracks. "Nova?" The woman from the night a few weeks ago stood in front of him. "What are you doing here?"

She pointed up at the building. "Same as you, I guess." Her eyes moved to Quinn. "I'm sorry, I didn't mean to bother you."

"You're no bother," Jesse said, "it's, um, it's really good to see you. This is my friend Quinn."

Nova smiled at her. "Hello there. Well, anyway, I should get going. I just saw you and wanted to say hello. I'll see you around." She waved her hand casually.

Jesse waved goodbye to her, feeling awkward. When she was far enough away that she could no longer hear them, Quinn spoke up. "Who was that?"

"Nova. She's...I met her at a bar a few weeks ago."

"What bar?" she asked, a half-smile on her face.

"When do you go to bars?" Suddenly her jaw dropped open. "Wait a second, by *met her at a bar*...do you mean *met* her at a bar?" Her nose scrunched up as if she'd smelled something bad. "As in you two..." she trailed off, the question in her eyes.

He lowered his voice. "It was the night before Reagan's wedding. We'd just lost a patient. I just...I don't know what happened."

"What is she? Like fifty?"

His voice grew defensive. "*No*. She's forty-five. Or something like that."

"Mhm," she said, looking unconvinced. "Why didn't you tell me?"

He shrugged. "I thought...I don't know. I thought you wouldn't want to know." They walked into a quiet room clad with Civil War era memorabilia.

"You thought I'd make fun of you, more likely." She grinned, running her fingers along the glass on one of the cases.

"Well, you are."

She spun around to face him. "I'm not making fun of you, Jess. I want you to be happy. You know that. I was just...I am *surprised* to see that the woman you've slept with is our parents' age. But, I'm even more surprised to find out that you hid it from me. That's not like you."

He took a deep breath, seeing the hurt in her expression. "I didn't tell you because the next time I saw you was the day of the wedding. And you looked...*so good*." She laughed off his compliment, but he continued. "I wasn't thinking about her. From the minute I walked through your door that night, I was thinking about you."

"Oh, what a line," she whispered, her eyes wide. Her gaze darted to the door as a group of people entered. She grabbed his hand, pulling him from the room. They passed three more crowded rooms without stopping before she found the large staircase. Still holding his hand, she led him up the stairs without a word. They looked down over the balcony as they reached the top.

"It wasn't a line," he said finally, turning his head to look at her.

"What are you talking about, Jess?" She eyed him, irritation in her voice. "What am I supposed to do with that?"

"What do you mean?"

"I mean," she paused, laughing under her breath and pinching the top of her nose. "You're my best friend. You can't say things like that to me."

"I didn't propose marriage, Quinn. I know you're adamantly against all forms of commitment. That doesn't mean I can't appreciate a beautiful woman in a dress, even if that woman happens to be you."

She rolled her eyes. "I'm not against all forms of commitment. I'm just not committing to the wrong guy."

"And you know the guys you go out with are wrong after one night?"

"Yes," she said stubbornly.

"How?"

"Because I know the right guy." Her cheeks turned red in a moment and he furrowed his brow at her, waiting for an explanation. "Hypothetically, I mean. I know what the right guy would be like."

"Oh, yeah, and what's that?" His heart began to race as studied her face while waiting for her to answer.

She snorted, crossing her hands in front of her and leaning out over the balcony, turning away from him. "Well, for starters, he's at least seventy."

TWELVE

JESSE
FOUR WEEKS LATER

"Brooks, Reed—you're with Garcia today. Buckley, you're helping to cover the pit. Dallas, I want you with Carter. Mathis, I'm putting you with Turner. No complaints," Janise Tedlock, the chief resident, informed the group. "We're running on a skeleton crew here today, guys. Any major tragedy happens and it's all hands on deck. So, let's work fast and efficient."

They nodded, the huddle adjourning. Jesse broke away from the group quickly, hurrying down the hall toward the women's wing. "Doctor Turner," he greeted the gray headed doctor. "Doctor Tedlock placed me on your service today."

"Great," he said, hardly acknowledging him as he handed over a stack of charts. "What year are you?"

"I'm," he paused, caught off guard by the question. "I'm a third year resident, sir."

"Great," he said again. "Have you done an abortion before?"

"I did three in medical school." He nodded. "None since I've been in residency."

"I've got one this morning. I'll let you take lead." He pointed to the door, leading him to the room. Jesse flipped through the charts, looking for the correct room number.

Doctor Turner knocked on the door before turning the handle. "Ms. Phillips, are you ready for us?"

"Yes," the voice answered before they could see her.

"This is Doctor Mathis, he'll be—"

"Jesse?" the woman on the table asked. He looked up from her chart just as he read her name. Jesse's breath caught in his chest, a lump rising in his throat. He couldn't speak.

"Do you two know each other?" the doctor asked, looking between them.

"Yeah," Jesse said, staring at Nova. "You could say that."

THIRTEEN

QUINN

Quinn sat across from her mother at the dinner table. "How have you been, Momma?"

Her mother nodded slowly. "I've been...okay," she said softly. "How's work?"

"Work is good. Busy." She ran her fork through her rice. "How's book club?"

"We haven't been meeting lately. Diane's been sick."

"Sick?"

"Just a cold, I think, but we didn't want to chance it last month."

"I hope she gets better," Quinn said, her voice quiet.

"Yes, well, the perks of having a husband as a doctor, I suppose. You can always get what you need. Not that I would know anymore." It was a dig at her father, but Quinn ignored it.

"You know, Doctor Norwood doesn't practice much

anymore. Not since he took over as chief. We actually hardly see him." Quinn was rambling, trying to make small talk. Since her father had left, things had become incredibly awkward around her mother, but she couldn't bear to leave her alone. She visited just about every other day.

"Yes, that's right, Diane had mentioned that," Shelly said, remembering. "Said he might retire a few years earlier than planned. Who knows, Quinnie, maybe someday you'll be there. You'd make a fantastic chief," she said, patting the table thoughtfully.

"Yes, maybe..." Quinn trailed off.

"How's Jesse?" her mother asked.

"He's doing okay. He's been pouring himself into work since the breakup, but I think he's finally starting to slow down."

Shelly reached up, patting her daughter's hand. "He's a good boy. He'll be okay."

Quinn smiled. "I think so too."

She took a deep breath, pulling her hand back. "Have you talked to your father lately?"

She frowned. "No, not in a few weeks. I think he's still in Cancun."

Her mother rolled her eyes.

"He'll be back," Quinn offered quietly. It was the subject they'd danced around for weeks: her father's sudden decision to skip town with a thirty-something red-headed nurse and leave his wife with little more than a note. Since his departure, they'd shared two phone calls. One where he offered a slight explanation— that he felt like Dale was suffocating him, his marriage was suffocating him, and he just needed some room to breathe. The other to ask for an account number of the electric bill that was coming due.

"And who says I'll want him back when he does? After he's run off with some teeny-bopper?" She scoffed, looking indignant.

"Well, you certainly don't have to do anything you don't want to. It's not like I'll blame you. I'm on your side in all of this."

Her mother wiped her forehead as if she were exhausted. "I don't want you to have to choose sides, sweetheart. I wanted you...I wanted us to be perfect for you. I wanted you to have the perfect family. I just wanted better for you than we've become." She lowered her head, her face full of pain.

"Momma," she whispered, leaning across the table. "You don't have to worry about that now. I'm raised. You're done. I had a perfect childhood." When her mother looked at her doubtingly, she raised her eyebrows. "I did. But, you don't have to be perfect for me anymore. Perfection isn't reality. I'm old enough to know that much."

"And what is that supposed to mean?"

"I just...I mean, there's no such thing as perfect. Damn sure not perfect love."

"Language," her mother warned. "And no, no relationship is perfect, but don't you dare tell me there's no such thing as perfect love. Love, true love, is the only thing in this world that is or ever could be perfect."

"You really still believe that? After everything?" Quinn pushed her plate away.

"I know it, Quinn. I know it in my bones. I believe it with all I have."

"But, Dad broke your heart." She stared down at the plate, at the uneaten noodles, finding herself unable to look her mom in the eye as she said it.

"He did," she said, matter-of-factly. "But your father is just one man. Powerful as he may be, he can't ruin love altogether. My love—my true love—is, and always has been, you."

She smiled, feeling cool tears brimming her eyes. "Momma—"

"Now, don't you 'momma' me." Shelly wiped her eyes quickly. "I still want you to go out and find a love of your own and then, eventually, a love like your father and I have for you." She smiled at her daughter, moving her hand to rub it over her cheek.

"Slow down there, Mom. I have to meet the guy first. I'd like a date or two before we decide on a beach or mountain house."

She laughed. "And how are we doing on that front?"

"Eh, not so hot." She shrugged.

Her mother poured herself more coffee from the pot sitting just behind her on the counter, stirring in a heap of creamer. "What about that nice boy you were seeing? The one with that ridiculous hat."

"The fedora? You mean Daniel? He's..." she trailed off, trying to find the right word to describe the lackluster week-long relationship she'd had with Daniel Kindall.

"He just...it wasn't going to go anywhere, Mom. And what is it with you and Jesse and this hat? The fedora wasn't so bad."

"Wearing a hat like that in a Georgia July, it's just pompous. I'm glad Jesse agrees. At least one of the boys you hang around with has some style. I've always liked him, you know." She winked, leaning back in her chair and resting her hands on her belly. Quinn couldn't help but notice that the roundness that had been there only a few short weeks ago was completely gone. Her father's departure had taken so much out of her mother.

"Yes, Jesse is the poster child for style and parental approval." She rolled her eyes, pretending to be annoyed, though a slight smile had crept on her face.

"Which is why you don't like him? Because you're such a rebel?"

"I love Jesse," she said, her tone serious. "But...yeah, he's a bit too perfect sometimes."

"There's no such thing as a perfect man."

She sighed, shaking her head. "Normally, I'd agree with you. But, I don't know, Mom. You should've seen him at that wedding. He was so reserved...calm...for lack of a better word, *perfect*. And it was all for her. He couldn't even see how awful it should have been. It was like I was the only one who could see how badly he was hurting. He'd even convinced himself he was fine. He couldn't see his pain because his only focus was being what she needed that day."

"Maybe. Or maybe...maybe he just wasn't hurting as much as you think he was. Maybe he wasn't putting on a show at all. Maybe his only focus was on the girl he brought with him, but she couldn't see that through all her own worry." Her mother gave her an all-knowing look.

She stared at her for a moment, wondering how she could possibly think such a ridiculous thing. "Mom, get real." She looked at her with a doubtful expression, her lips pursed. "Jesse is my best friend. He has been since we were running around in diapers. He doesn't see me like that, trust me. It'd be way too weird."

"Says who?"

She recited the reason in her head as she'd rehearsed it. "Says every failed friendship-turned-lovers-turned-enemies story ever told. We wouldn't risk our friendship. It's too important. *He's* too important."

Her mother smiled and Quinn could swear she saw a small tear in her eye. "Whatever you say, Quinnie. But, nobody writes books about friendships, beautiful as they may be. Nobody flocks to the theater to watch a movie about great pals, though they might have the most amazing adventures. Friends can change your life, maybe even save your life if given the chance, but love...oh, the best kind of love...well, that might just *give you* life."

FOURTEEN

JESSE

"Nova, what are you doing here?" he asked once Doctor Turner had shut the door, leaving them alone.

"You mean this isn't where I go to get a wax?" She feigned being disappointed.

"You're here for an abortion?"

"Congrats, doc, you can read."

"Since when are you pregnant?" He pulled out her chart, flipping through it. "You're...eight weeks?" He sat down on the rolling stool, running his hands over his forehead. "Oh my god. Oh my god," he repeated, his thoughts wild.

"Hey, now, if I'd known you were going to be here, there's no way I would've come. I didn't even know you were a doctor, hell I didn't even know your last name, let alone that you worked here. Don't go panicking on me."

"Eight weeks," he repeated, trying to do the math in

his head. *Eight weeks since her last period, six weeks, give or take, since they'd had sex.* "Oh my god." He began hyperventilating. "Is it...I mean...oh my god. Is...you're pregnant? We—did I? Is it mine? *You're pregnant?*"

She glanced at the clock on the wall. "Only for an hour longer."

"How can you be so callous about this? Weren't you even going to tell me? Don't I have a right to know?" He wasn't sure what the feeling was that had suddenly filled him. Anger? Fear, maybe?

"Not unless *you* plan on carrying it," she said, crossing her arms.

"Look, I'm all for women's rights, but that's still my child. Don't you think I deserved to at least know?"

"Meaning what? Why would you want to know? Just to upset you? Because I don't have time for that. I have to be back at work tonight."

"Don't you think I have rights? I may not be able to carry that child, but I am the father. I am, right?"

"Yeah," she said with a nod. "Yeah, you are the father. So, what Jesse? You want it?"

"I—I don't know. But it'd be nice to at least be allowed the choice."

She held her hands in the air. "Thank you. That's what every woman has been screaming for the past hundred years."

"I don't know what I want, Nova," he said, "but I know I don't want this." He gestured to her lying on the table.

"What about what I want? I'm forty-eight years old.

I'm divorced. I finally have my life all to myself. You said you don't know what you want, well let me be perfectly clear about what I don't want: I *don't* want a kid. I *don't* want to be a mom. And I certainly don't want to raise any babies with a boy who's barely more than a baby himself."

He started to argue about his age but refrained. "*Can you just*...just give me a second to process this? Please?" He took a deep breath. "Can I see it?" he asked quietly, trying to collect his raging thoughts.

"What? No." She looked as though his question were absurd.

"Please, Nova. If you'll let me, I'd really like to see it. Just once." When she didn't answer, he spoke again. "I'm asking you to let me see our baby."

"It's tissue," she whispered, but he saw the glimmer of vulnerability in her eyes then.

"You don't have to look," he said softly, walking to her bed. "Please. Please just let me see."

She tightened her mouth, looking away but making no effort to protest as he lifted her gown and put the warm gel on her lower belly. He placed the transducer probe onto her skin, searching for her uterus. Within an instant, there it was. The baby. A small clump of cells attached to her uterine wall. Tears burned his eyes as he saw it wiggle. Once, twice, then once more for good measure. *I'm here,* it seemed to say. He stared at the screen, at the tiny white dot that might someday have his nose.

It was too soon to hear the heartbeat, but he could see it...a steady one-hundred-fifty-four beats per minute.

Healthy. Strong. He watched the heart chambers fluttering on the screen, mesmerized.

Beside him, she cleared her throat. He pulled the probe away, looking down. Her eyes were on him—not the screen, but no longer on the far wall either. He knew she could see the tears in his eyes, but he didn't dare wipe them.

"Is it healthy?" she asked, so quiet he almost didn't hear it.

"Perfectly," he answered too fast. He walked to the end of her bed, taking a seat and preparing himself to beg for what had quickly become the most important thing in the world to him.

"Will it hurt?" she asked, interrupting his thoughts. "The abortion, I mean?" So, he realized, she was still going through with it. Her words burned his chest, but he tried to keep his face still. He cleared his throat, careful not to let his voice crack.

"We will give you medicine for the pain. You'll be awake for the whole procedure since you're still under twelve weeks, but we'll keep you comfortable. You might feel a bit of pressure and some discomfort after it's over. We will give you a prescription to make it bearable, though any over the counter pain reliever will work."

She nodded, staring at her hands in her lap. "I'm sorry I didn't tell you. I didn't think you'd care."

"Of course I care," he said, standing up again and staring at her with concern.

Still not looking at him, she went on. "You have your whole life ahead of you. Don't let me ruin that." Her feet swung awkwardly, bouncing off the metal of the examination table.

He shook his head. "You've got it all wrong, Nova. A baby wouldn't ruin my life. I promise you it wouldn't. You don't have to do this. And especially not to protect me."

"You aren't allowed to talk me out of it. You're my doctor. I know my rights." Her voice grew louder as she finally looked up at him.

He held his hands up, taking a step back. "I'm not going to talk you out of it. I can't, you're right. It's your body, your right to choose. And I do respect that. Let me be clear, Nova: I'm not anti-abortion. I'm anti-*this*-abortion. Because this abortion is every bit mine as it is yours. And I will feel that loss just as much as you will. So, no, I won't talk you out of it. That's not fair of me. But what I will do is let you know your options. And I'll beg you to reconsider based on the option I'm giving you. Because even if you don't want this baby...which is totally fair...I do. And I'll take it. I'll take care of it. I'll take care of everything. Medical bills, the baby, you, whatever you need...I'll do it. I'll do everything I can." He paused, staring into her dark eyes. "I just can't carry it. The rest is on me. Just give me seven months. Seven more months, and I'll do anything you want."

Her eyes were pure stone. "And if I say no?"

"There's nothing I can do to stop you. I will have to excuse myself from your case though, either way. I can't be your doctor. Not under these circumstances."

"You said twelve weeks, right? I'm only eight. I still have time to decide?"

His heart leapt. "Yes, you do."

She leaned forward, crossing her hands over her legs. "Okay. Four weeks to prove you can do this."

"Thank you," he said, adrenaline coursing through him. "I promise you I can."

"But, Jess?" she said as tears began to cloud his vision once again.

"Yeah?"

"This won't be a happy ending kind of story. Not for us, anyway. You might get your baby, but you'll be raising it alone. I won't change my mind about that. I just want to make sure I'm clear. This baby is not in my plans and I won't change them for anyone. Not ever again."

He touched her hand cautiously. "I won't ask you for anything else. This baby is the only happy ending I need."

FIFTEEN

QUINN

Quinn walked into her house, surprised to see the television light flickering from the living room. She set her bag down on the bench and hung her keys up.

"Jess?" she called out to the only person who should have her key, tiptoeing across the hardwood. He was on the couch, his head hung back, jaw wide open. She approached him cautiously, sliding her hand onto his shoulder as she sank into the couch. He stirred, his eyes opening slightly. "Jess?" she whispered, rubbing a thumb over the crease in his forehead.

He opened his eyes, jumping back an inch before he seemed to realized where he was.

"What are you doing here?" she asked, a smile on her face.

"What time is it?" He yawned, stretching his arms above his head.

"It's after two."

"I thought you had an early shift."

"I got stuck in surgery," she said. "Do you want to eat with me? I can order out."

"Pizza's in the fridge," he said. "I planned to wait for you, but I got hungry. And then, apparently, I got tired too."

She sighed, standing up, but sat back down in an instant. His eyes were off, a light missing in them somehow. "Is everything okay?"

"Go ahead and get changed. It can wait until you've eaten," he told her.

She shook her head, crossing one leg over the other and leaning back. "Not a chance. What's going on?"

He took a deep breath, his eyes dancing between hers. She pressed her lips together, bracing herself for the blow of whatever must be coming. He opened his mouth, though no words came out. Finally, his head shook, his eyes blinking heavily.

"What is it, Jess? You're scaring me," she said, trying to keep her voice light.

"I'm going to be a dad."

His words hit her hard, words that in a million years she could've never expected. "What?" she asked, though she wasn't sure if the word even came out.

"I...it's a crazy story, actually." A slight smile filled his face as he ran his palm through his blond hair.

"Crazy like you got a lobotomy and this is all a joke?" She could only hope.

"No."

"Jess, I'm confused. Start talking now." Could he see her hands shaking? Her stomach was suddenly balled into a knot.

"It's that woman you met at the gardens. Nova."

"The old one?" The air around her grew tight, chills lining her arms. "Can she even *get* pregnant?" She felt as though she were going to be sick.

"Obviously," he said, holding his hands out in front of him in shock. "I don't know. I'm so caught off guard by all of this, too."

"So, what are you going to do?" she asked the question she wasn't sure she wanted to know the answer to.

"I don't know," he said, his voice shaking. She pulled him into a hug, rubbing his back. They remained still for a moment and she let go.

"Do you want her to keep it? Does she want to? Are you even sure it's yours?"

He shook his head. "I mean, she said it is, and she'd have no reason to lie. She wasn't asking for anything from me. The timing lines up. But, I don't honestly know. She doesn't want to keep it anyway. She was planning to have an abortion. I just...I couldn't let her do it."

She sat still for a moment, processing. When she spoke, her voice was soft, careful. "You couldn't *let* her? You stopped her from getting an abortion? Jess, you can't—"

"I didn't stop her. I let her know that she had other options," he interrupted.

She eyed him, the sickly feeling not going away. "So, what does that mean?"

He looked at her, his eyes wild with fear. "I don't know, Q. I said I would keep it. That I'll do it on my own, if she'll just change her mind about the abortion."

"And what did she say?" She spoke slowly.

"I mean, she didn't have it today, but she said she needs time to figure everything out."

"She's...old, Jess," she said.

"Forty-eight isn't—"

She held her hand up when he started to defend her. "I don't say that to be mean because in the grand spectrum of life...no, forty-eight isn't old. But, forty-eight in childbearing years, that's...geriatric pregnancy. The risks will be super high. There's a good chance the pregnancy could be a danger to the baby or Nova, or both."

"I know that," he said. "And I knew that when I asked her to keep the baby. But...I don't know. I just...I couldn't let her go through with it. Not unless she knew she had a different choice." He was quiet for a moment. "Does that make me selfish?"

She leaned into his shoulder, propping her feet up on the small coffee table. "I don't know."

"She said she won't help me with the baby. Even if she decides to have it, she's going to hand it over and walk away. And I'm...I'm a surgeon. I have a crazy schedule. I know nothing at all about babies. What am I supposed to do, though? I just couldn't let her go through with it. I know none of it makes sense, I know I'm getting myself in over my head. Logically, I know this is a terrible decision." He nodded to himself, his gaze locked on the floor.

She ran her hand over his chest, clutching his fingers. "But none of this is about logic," she said.

He shook his head, his stubble scraping her forehead. "No, I guess not."

She felt a tear touch her scalp, but she didn't dare move. "It's going to be okay, Jess," she said, her fingers intertwined with his. "You know we'll figure this out."

"I don't know if that's true. What if I just make this kid's life a mess? What if I'm a total failure?"

"What if you aren't?" she asked, looking up at him. "What if you give this kid a life it wouldn't have had if you hadn't stopped her? What if you give him a shot?"

"I can't do this alone, Quinn," he said. "I have no idea what I'm doing."

Seeing him break in front of her was more than she could take. She leaned in, pressing her cheek into his cheek, their faces smashed together. She wrapped a palm around the back of his neck. "You know there's no way you're ever going to be alone in anything you do," she told him.

His lips brushed her cheek, finding a tear that had slipped out. He pulled back, his breath warm on her face. "I can't ask you to help me. This isn't your mess."

"You're my mess, Jess. You always have been. And you aren't asking."

"What would I ever do without you?" he asked, his chest swelling, eyes warming.

"Lucky you, you'll never have to find out," she whispered, her eyes locked on his. Her pulse sped up, watching his eyes search hers. Their hands locked together once again as he leaned forward, his lips parting. The room stood still, the air around them silent as his mouth landed on hers.

It was careful, at first, his lips resting together calmly. She couldn't stop the breath that escaped her nose. She felt his mouth opening, his tongue brushing against her lips, and she knew she was close to giving in to everything she'd always wanted. She was frozen, trapped between an overwhelming happiness and an ice cold fear that this could only end badly.

His hands moved to her face, his thumbs caressing her cheeks. He pulled away from her. "I don't know what I'm doing," he whispered, their noses still touching. He waited for her response.

"Jesse, I—" she started, but she wasn't sure what to say.

"Should I stop?" His face moved further back.

"I—I just think you're upset. I don't want you to do something you'd regret." She bit her lip.

He pressed his forehead into hers. "I'm sorry," he said before leaning back into the couch, the moment over.

"You don't have to be sorry, Jess. I know you're having a rough time right now." She tried desperately to keep her breathing steady.

"Yeah, I guess so," he said, looking away.

"I'm gonna go change," she said, standing up. He nodded, not saying another word.

When she returned, minutes later, he was already back asleep. She sighed, cursing her self-sabotaging behavior. She should've let him kiss her, let them finally explore what had been hanging in the air between them for years—but the moment wasn't right. It was a moment she'd dreamed of for so long, a night she'd imagined so many times, but with the revelation of the baby she couldn't allow his vision, *or decision,* to be clouded by anything. Least of all, her. Jesse was most important. About that, her feelings would never change.

SIXTEEN

JESSE

Jesse and Nova sat at a cafe just outside of Dale. They'd been there for an hour, avoiding the inevitable. He was currently trying to convince her to meet his parents when he told them their news.

"I just don't think it's a good idea, Jesse. I don't belong there."

"I get that you feel that way, and I understand why. But it's important to me that you see that I'm capable of taking care of this baby. My family is my support system. They'll play a big role in our baby's life."

"*Your* baby," she corrected.

"Right," he said, "but I just feel like you should see where it'll end up."

"It'll be with you and not me. I'm sorry, but that's really all I care about," she said, her face stern.

"You might change your mind," he insisted. "It's possible."

"Don't try to change my mind, Jesse. I won't budge. I do not want this baby, plain and simple. I'm giving you a chance to have it, because I'm not a complete monster, but that doesn't mean I'll come around to anything else. My mind is made up."

"That's fine," he said hurriedly. He couldn't help feeling like he was walking on eggshells with her. Saying or doing the wrong thing could cost him his child. "I just thought it would be nice."

"And what would your parents think, anyway? About the fact that you knocked up someone their age?"

He let out a breath. "Trust me, they'll be more in shock about the pregnancy than about your age." He hoped that was true, at least.

She frowned. "What are their names, anyway? Oh my god, I probably know them." She placed her head in her hands, sighing.

"That's right," he said, realization hitting him. "You're from Dale. You probably do. Oh, wow." He exhaled loudly, panic beginning to set in.

"Jesse?" Nova asked.

"Right." He shook his head quickly. "Their, um, their names are Jim—James Mathis and Cherie. Mom was an Almaroad before she got married."

Nova's face went ghastly white, her eyes wide. She looked down at her mug of decaf coffee.

"And based on that face, I'm...guessing you know them?" he asked.

"Your father is *James Mathis?* Big Jim? The freaking mayor of Dale?"

He would've given anything for her to say that the names hadn't sounded familiar, but he could almost guarantee that wouldn't be the case. Everyone in Dale knew everyone. And Big Jim was practically Dale's own celebrity. "Umm, yeah," he answered finally.

"Why wouldn't you tell me that?" she demanded, her tone clipped.

"I didn't know it was relevant." He lowered his brow.

"You're small town royalty, Jesse. Of course it's relevant." She groaned, rolling her forehead in her palms. "I was in your parent's graduating class. Literally, I'm the exact same age. I remember when your parents announced they were pregnant with you." Panic began to fill her voice, her breathing growing rapid. "And now I'm knocked up by that baby. Oh my god, what have I done?" She was reaching hysterics. "Jesse, what the hell were we thinking? This is so stupid. We are...oh god, we're so stupid." She slammed her hand on the table in frustration.

"Nova, calm down," he said. "Everything's going to be okay. Age is just a number, after all. This was a decision we both made. You didn't force me into anything. Just breathe, okay?" He reached out his hand, taking hers. "If anything, maybe my parents will take comfort in the fact that they know you."

She looked skeptical. "Somehow I doubt that, but I appreciate your optimism. I'm sorry, Jesse. I just can't go with you. I have to go." She let go of his hand, standing up and grabbing her coat and purse from the seat beside her.

"Nova, wait!" he called after her. "Wait!" The restaurant patrons had begun looking at them, frowning at the commotion, and his pride prevented him from yelling anymore as she hurried out the door.

He followed her to her car, stopping only when she pulled out of her parking spot rapidly. She slowed down, lowering her window slightly.

"Nova, please." He put his hands together as if in prayer. "Please...please don't make any decisions because of who my family is. Or because you're embarrassed or worried about what people will think. Because I don't care. I don't care what anyone thinks about us or this baby." His voice cracked as he pleaded with her.

She spoke through the crack between her window and the frame, staring at her hands on the wheel. "I'm not going to have an abortion just because I don't want to meet your family, Jesse. I'm not worried about what your parents will think or embarrassed by their opinions. I couldn't care less what anyone in that town thinks anymore. I just...I don't want to be involved. There is no 'us' and me meeting your family would only point to the contrary. I want to be as uninvolved as possible. But, you'll still get your baby."

He took a step forward. "Thank you."

She hesitated, but finally looked his way, rolling the window down a bit more. "You're a good guy, Jesse. I don't want to hurt you."

"Can I see you again?" he asked, placing his hand on the glass.

"I don't know if that's a good idea." She looked away again.

"We're going to have to get you some doctor's appointments scheduled. I'd like to be a part of that, if you'll let me. It would really mean a lot."

She bit her lip, huffing. "Okay."

"Okay?"

"I'll let you go with me to appointments if you want, but you have to set everything up." She turned her head slightly so he could see her face once again. Her sad expression made his throat feel tight.

"I will," he said. "I'll take care of everything."

"And Jesse?"

"Yeah?"

"We aren't going to be able to see each other outside of appointments. I don't want anyone to get confused about what our relationship is."

He nodded, knowing she was talking about him more than anyone else. "I understand."

"Goodbye, Jesse," she said, rolling her window back up.

"Take care of yourself," he said, "both of you." He frowned, standing still long after she'd driven off.

SEVENTEEN

JESSE

"I need you," Jesse said urgently the second her voice rang out over the line.

"I'm at work, Jess. What's wrong?" Quinn asked.

"She won't come with me."

"Who won't come—Nova won't?"

"No," he said, "I have to tell my parents. I'm twenty-eight years old. I'm an adult. So, why the hell am I nervous?"

"Because you don't want to disappoint them." She always seemed to understand him. Her voice was echoing suddenly, and he realized she must've stepped into a supply closet or empty on-call room.

"Well, that's inevitable at this point," he said, trying to sound cavalier.

"Jess, you said it. You're twenty-eight years old. They can't change your mind or ground you or punish you.

They can be mad at you, but that's not going to change what's happening. You just have to remember that. Your life is yours. I know you're so used to doing everything right, but I promise you the world isn't going to end over this. Everything's going to be okay."

"How can you promise that?"

"Because I won't let it be anything else." He smiled, feeling relief wash over him, though she'd made no real promise. "You know I'm always here for you, right?" she asked softly.

"I know," he said.

"Do you need me to come with you to your parents?"

"No," he answered immediately, but changed his mind. "Would I be the worst best friend ever if I said yes?"

She laughed. "Never."

"They like you," he explained. "There's less chance of them killing me if you're there."

"Fair enough. I'll bring a tarp just in case." She laughed under her breath. Her wit was something Jesse never failed to be entertained by, though this time his nervousness prevented him from laughing along with her. "When are you planning on telling them?"

"Tonight. When do you get off? Mom'll be home after the bank closes, usually around four or five."

She was quiet. He could hear her breathing into the speaker as she seemed to be moving. "Okay," she said finally, "I can be there by five."

"Thank you, Quinn. I owe you one."

She laughed again, her laugh warming him. "I'll hold you to it, Mathis. *Shoot,* I gotta go. Tedlock is paging me."

With that, the line went dead. His heart fell at no longer hearing her voice. Lately, she was the only thing that seemed to put a smile on his face. *What in the world was happening to them?* Since the night of the wedding, his feelings for Quinn were all over the place. He shook his head, as if to shake the thoughts out. They were best friends. Had been since birth practically. No way in hell could he afford to lose her. Of course, much to his dismay, that also meant he could never afford to have her.

EIGHTEEN

JESSE

"Well, dig in," Cherie told them, holding out the dish of pasta for Quinn. "I'm so glad you could join us, sweetheart. I feel like we never see you anymore."

Quinn smiled. "Thanks, Mrs. Mathis."

"Yeah, it's 'bout time we had someone with some class around here," Big Jim joked, elbowing Jesse. He wasn't sure if it was a jab at himself or Reagan.

"Mom, Dad," Jesse said, his voice leaving his throat before he was entirely ready. His hands were cold as ice, sweat beading on his palms. Quinn set the dish down awkwardly beside him. "I actually needed to talk to you guys about something."

His parents put down their silverware, looking between him and Quinn.

"Well," Big Jim coaxed, "what is it?"

"I, um, well...I...it's going to be a shock, what I'm going to tell you, I mean. It wasn't really in any of our plans, I know. But I'm really okay with it. And I want you to be okay with it, too."

"What are you talking about, son? Okay with what?" Cherie asked.

"Mom..." he started, his eyes locked on hers. Her perfect image of him was about to be shattered, and that was killing him. "I—I'm going to have a baby."

Both parents immediately looked to Quinn.

"What?" his father asked.

"You're pregnant?" Cherie stood up from her chair, her voice high. The question was directed at Quinn.

"*No!*" Jesse and Quinn both exclaimed at the same time, Quinn's hands on her belly as if protecting her uterus from getting any ideas.

"No, it's not Quinn," Jesse assured them, surprised to see no anger in their eyes. He cast a small smile her way and she smirked. "She's just here as a friend."

"Well, then what's going on?" Cherie asked, hands on her hips. "Not that Reagan? You've been broken up too long."

"No, not Reagan either," Jesse assured them. "You don't know her. Er, well, you do. It's complicated—"

"That's putting it lightly," Quinn mumbled under her breath.

"We aren't dating—the mother and I—it was just a one night thing. We're both really surprised, but I want to make the best of it."

His mother placed her hand on her chest. "A...one night thing? Jess, we raised you better than that." She spoke as though the news had taken her breath away. "How could you do something so senseless?"

"It's not something I *do,* Mom. Usually, I'm...I mean," he stopped, not wanting to go into details with his mom about his somewhat un-exciting sex life. "It was a bad night. And, I know, that's the lamest excuse out there, but it's the truth. I'd been dumped, we'd lost a patient at work, and I was really struggling." He looked to Quinn again, who was now avoiding eye contact. She twirled her fork around on her plate aimlessly. "It doesn't really matter though—the why of it all. It's done and happening. I just wanted you to hear it from me."

His mother covered her mouth, tears welling in her eyes.

"Mom, please don't cry," he said, cocking his head to the side.

"Who is she?" Big Jim asked.

"Her name's Novalee," he said, bracing himself for the most uncomfortable part of the conversation.

"Novalee who? You said we know her? Is she from Dale?" his father inquired, looking serious.

"I, um," he paused, realizing with embarassment he didn't even know her last name. He tried to recall what her chart had said. He felt the heat rushing to his face.

"The only Novalee we know is Novalee Phillips, but she's our age," his mother said, as if that were the most ridiculous idea ever. "So, it can't be her."

He looked down, pressing his lips together. "That would be her," he said, raising his eyes slightly.

The room fell silent. His parents, his mother's complexion gone white while his father's grew red, stared at him in disbelief. "I know what you must be thinking," he said, though he genuinely hoped he didn't. "It certainly wasn't—"

"Stop talking," Big Jim's voice thundered through the room. "Novalee Phillips is not going to be having your baby."

"What?" Jesse looked at his father. "What is that supposed to mean?"

"We'll give you the money to make this go away," his father responded, ignoring his mother as a cry escaped her throat. "And you *will* make this go away. This is not going to happen."

"What are you talking about?" Jesse pushed his chair back from the table. "I know you aren't suggesting I have her get an abortion? Or pay her off? Because that's absolutely not your call. This is my child we're talking about." His own voice grew louder as his father's rage seemed to intensify.

Big Jim stood up, joining Cherie. "You don't know Novalee Phillips like we do, son. You don't know what we know. I'll only repeat myself once, Jesse: it's not going to happen. You need to get out of this, whatever way you can. Novalee is trouble, bad news. She's not the type of person I'll have my son associating with."

Jesse looked to his mother, hoping for her support,

but she clasped Big Jim's hand, nodding sadly. "Your father's right, Jesse. We can't let you go through with this."

"You may run this town, but you don't run my life. You don't have to *let* me do anything. I'm having this baby. With Nova. So, if you don't like it...then I guess you don't. But, it won't change reality."

His father's face went from red to purple, seemingly at a loss for words.

"I'm going to excuse us now," Jesse said, "before you embarrass me any more. It's obvious I'm not going to get the support I'd hoped for from either of you." He stood up, holding out his hand for Quinn's. She took it cautiously.

"Jesse, don't leave like this," his mother called after him.

"Let him go, Cherie," his dad bellowed, towering over them as he pulled Quinn from the room.

"Thank you for dinner, Mr. and Mrs. Mathis," Quinn said as they disappeared from the dining room, though they all knew she'd eaten none.

Jesse's pulse was racing, anger flooding him. They made it through the living room and out the door in a second. Quinn grabbed both of their coats, throwing hers over her shoulders as he shut the door.

He looked up at the sky, groaning, placing the inside of his fist to his forehead. "I don't know what I was thinking."

"What? With Nova?"

"With my parents." He could see their breath in the air, though his body was on fire with rage.

"They just need time to—"

The door opened and his mother stepped out.

"I'm not coming back in," Jesse told her angrily before she could speak.

"I think that's best right now," she said simply, surprising him. "Jess, there's something you should know about Novalee before you make any decisions."

"I've already decided, Mom. I don't even know if she'll be involved in the baby's life. I may be doing it all on my own. But, I'm doing it either way. Decision made."

His mother pressed her fingers to her lips. "What do you mean?"

"If Dad had let me finish in there, I would've had the chance to tell you. Nova isn't interested in the baby. I'm the only thing keeping her from doing exactly what Dad wants. My hope is that she's just in shock and she'll eventually come around to the idea, but I'm not holding my breath. Right now, this is all on me."

"Oh, Jess," she said. He could see the reflection of the porch light in the small tears that were cascading down her cheeks. "I'm so sorry," she whispered. "I'm so sorry about all of this." She leaned forward, touching his shoulder.

"I'm not sad, Mom. I'm honestly okay with all of this. I mean, I'm shocked but I've had time to process. I'm going to be okay. There's no need to be sorry. But I do wish you and Dad would be more supportive of my decisions, even if you don't understand them."

She shook her head. "I just wish I could protect you."

"Protect me from what?"

Another tear fell from her eye and she moved to wipe it. "Just...don't get your hopes up about the baby. Not until it's here." She spoke quietly, as if it were a secret.

"What does that mean?"

"Your father doesn't think we should tell you, but I disagree. It seems fair for you to have all the information before you to decide to move forward."

"I've already decided to—"

"*Just* hear me out," his mother said forcefully.

"Okay, go ahead," he said, crossing his arms. He could hear Quinn shuffling around behind him—a nervous habit of hers.

"Back when we were young, around the time that I was pregnant with you, there were rumors that Novalee Phillips had gotten pregnant, too."

"What?" Shock resonated through him. Why hadn't she told him?

"Let me finish, Jess. It makes me sick to even have to tell it, so just let me get through." She covered her mouth as though she might be physically sick any minute.

He nodded, swallowing hard. The air was thick with anticipation. He felt Quinn's hand touching his back, her presence calming him only slightly.

"Rumor had it that she was pregnant by a married man. After a few months, she was showing, and despite her outright denial and the questions about the father, we all knew the pregnancy rumors had to be true."

"She had a kid?"

"Jesse, stop interrupting," she instructed him. "When she was around seven or eight months along, Novalee was found in an alley unconscious and bleeding. Doctor Norwood and your father," she said, looking to Quinn, "worked on her for hours, but the baby was gone. There was nothing they could do to save it."

"What happened to her? She was attacked?"

He heard Quinn suck in a breath similar to his own as his mother answered. "No, Jesse, she'd given herself a DIY abortion. They said she tried to cut the baby out." His mother looked as though she might faint, but she continued talking. "Rumor had it that the father had refused to leave his wife and Novalee was acting out. She killed her own child because of some spat between them."

"I think I'm going to be sick," Quinn whispered.

Jesse stood still, unable to move. Could what his mother was saying be true? What reason would she have to lie like this?

"I'm only telling you this because you need to understand how unstable she is. If you decide to open your heart to this baby, the slightest thing could cause you to set her off...and it could cost you everything. I'm telling you this because I wish I could spare you the heartache that you're inevitably going to go through falling in love with a baby that will rely on Novalee's sanity to stay alive." His mother's face was dark. She leaned forward, kissing his cheek. "Now, I'm going to go inside. Your father and I will be here when you make your decision, and we will support whatever decision that is. But, your heartache is our heartache...just remember that." She said, her lips pressed together in a grimace. "You'll never be alone in this, Jesse. But, that won't make it hurt any less."

With that, she turned and walked into the house without another word.

NINETEEN

QUINN

Back at Quinn's house, they laid on her bed. Jesse hadn't spoken a word in nearly an hour.

"It's going to be okay," she whispered for the thirteenth time that night. He shook his head. "Jesse, please talk to me." ،

Again, his head shook. "What am I supposed to do, Quinn? Do I...do I confront her? Do I ask her if it's true? And what if it is? What then?" Questions that must've been filling his thoughts poured out of him.

"What can you do if it is true?" she asked. He looked at her. "Will you want the baby any less?"

He shrugged. "Of course not."

"Then what she did in her past doesn't matter. What matters is seeing her through this pregnancy and getting your child, Jess. After that, you can figure the rest out."

"Do you think it's true?" he asked, his expression withdrawn, his eyes dark.

"I don't know." She bit her lip, touching her cheeks with her palms. "I hope not. But, we've all done horrible, stupid things as kids, right? She could be a totally different person than she was...what, twenty-some years ago. Don't judge her for her past," she warned him. "Just take care of what you can and don't dwell on what you can't."

He pulled her over onto his chest, rubbing her hair. "When did you get to be so smart?"

"I'm not...okay, I am smart, but it's not brains that's getting me through this situation, Jesse. It's heart. I've seen people at their worst. We both have. People come to us, broken and hopeless and sometimes even evil, and we don't get to judge. We just heal. We heal and let them move on with their lives. And that's all I'm doing right now. I'm just trying to...cauterize the wound and wait for it to heal."

He kissed the top of her head. "You're amazing, you know that?"

She looked up at him. "Yeah, I know." She smiled, her cheeks pulling back to reveal all her teeth. It seemed as though it had been so long since she smiled so big, but she could see how much he needed a bit of happiness. "You're going to be an outstanding father, Jesse. You were great with Nora. This baby is lucky to have you."

"I don't know about that."

"I mean it," she said, placing her hand on his chest to prop herself up. "You know what you're doing is a good thing, right? It's one of the most selfless things I've ever seen anyone do." She paused. "I'm really proud of you."

His eyes danced between hers, his hands moving to hold her arms. A piece of his blond hair was blowing in the breeze from her fan, making her want to reach out and run her hands through it. He moved his lips, his tongue grazing the top one. His cheeks had a flush to them she hadn't noticed before. "Jess?" she asked.

"Shhh," he quieted her, his breathing erratic. He leaned in, his eyes watching hers as he moved closer to her mouth. She was quiet, her wild eyes on his. His nose touched hers, their mouths only inches apart. His warm breath hit her cheek, causing heat to fill her body. He took a breath and leaned his chin in so that his mouth was resting on hers.

His kiss was soft, his lips parting only slightly. She tilted her head, still in complete shock about what was happening. His hands gripped her arms tighter, though not rough, and his palms slid over her skin. He reached her shoulders and then her face, his hands holding her cheeks as his tongue entered her mouth.

She tensed, wanting to stop but unable to speak. He wrapped his arms around her waist, pulling her up so that she was straddling him. His kiss was so familiar, yet foreign all at once. *It was her best friend causing her heart to accelerate, her best friend causing the blush on her skin.* She couldn't stop the thoughts from rushing through her mind. But, no matter how weird she consciously knew this situation was, her subconscious seemed to have other plans. She moved her hands to his scalp, her hands running through his thick hair.

Finally, he pulled back, catching his breath. His forehead still remained locked with hers. "I'm sorry," he said.

She jerked back. "Sorry?" she asked.

"Not about kissing you." His lips were bright red as he spoke, and she couldn't help herself staring at them. "But for not doing it sooner."

"Jesse," she said, rubbing a thumb over his cheek as her hands slid down from his hair. "This is...dangerous."

"I know," he said. "I don't know why I'm feeling this way."

"What way?" she asked, curiosity filling her.

"It's like," he said, groaning as he ran a hand over his face.

"Tell me," she begged.

"It's like...ever since that night. The night of the wedding, I look at you and you're the same girl, the same skinny little thirteen-year-old Quinn that played in my yard all those years ago, and yet...I'm seeing you as this whole new person." His eyes grew wide. "This whole new woman. And, I just can't help but want to keep doing this." He ran his hands over her arms quickly as if he were warming her up, his gaze traveling from her lips to her eyes and back. "It's the craziest thing."

"I know," she said, agreeing. For her, the moment had come years ago. The moment she'd finally seen Jesse for who he was. A man. A man who could make her knees weak and her heart flutter with very little effort.

"You do?"

She nodded. "I do."

"So, what does this mean?" he asked. "I mean, you're...you're *Quinn*. You're my best friend." He took her hand in his. "And I'm...my life is so complicated right now."

She went to move off his lap, realizing what he was saying. "This doesn't have to mean anything. We can forget it happened."

He took hold of her hips, stopping her from leaving. "I don't want to forget," he told her. He leaned forward, kissing her again. "I want to remember. I want—" He gave her another kiss. "Every minute of this ingrained into my memory."

She smiled, tucking a piece of hair behind her ear. "But, this is complicated. We can't forget that."

"No, we can't. And the most important thing to me, Quinn, is that I don't lose you. So, we have to be careful. Whatever we decide, wherever we go from here...I can't lose you." He brushed the piece of her hair back behind her ear as it fell free again.

She kissed his forehead, sliding off his lap and laying beside him. "I don't want to lose you either, Jesse. You're the only thing that keeps me sane most days."

"So, what do we do?" he asked, crossing his legs and staring at her.

"I wish I knew," she whispered. "I really do."

"What do you want to do?"

She looked up at him, surprised by the question. "Meaning?"

"Meaning what do you want to do? Do you want what we are to change?"

"No," she answered honestly. "I don't want our friendship to change, Jesse. Because it's the only constant I have. But, that doesn't mean I don't want...I don't know, *more* with you."

"More?" he asked, his eyebrows shooting up.

"Stop making me do all the talking," she said, trying to hide the embarrassment she felt. "What do you want?"

"I want to hear more about this *more,*" he told her.

"Jesse, I'm serious." She rolled over, propping her head up on her pillow. "What do you want from me? From us?"

"I don't know," he said. "God, I wish I did. What I do know is that I love you. Like I always have. But, my feelings for you are changing. In a way that I never thought possible. And, that kiss—I mean, I never thought I could kiss you like that. I never knew I could *want* to kiss you like that. I feel like a kid again, getting all nervous about my feelings. But, with you it's different. Because above all, our friendship means the most to both of us."

"Can we ever just go back to being friends after this?" she asked the question she knew must be weighing on both of their minds. "I mean, these feelings that you're having for me, are they romantic? Is it just lust?"

"It's not just lust," he said, looking away.

"I don't want this to be some rebound thing," she said, wagging her finger at him.

He laughed under his breath, moving a finger under her chin and lifting it to him. "I haven't thought about

Reagan in weeks, honestly. I'm not rebounding. And I would *never* do that with you. You're too important to me, Quinn."

"So, then what does that mean?"

He sighed. "I think it means whatever we used to have...everything is about to change. I don't know if there's anything we can do to stop that now." She gulped, knowing he was right. "And that really scares me."

"Me too."

He pulled the covers out, sliding under them and allowing her to as well. "Come here," he said, and fear consumed her. What would happen between them? Quinn's body shook with anticipation. Seeing the look on her face, his expression changed. "Roll over," he whispered, reaching behind him and flipping off the light. "Nothing has to change tonight." She did as she was told, scooting back until she felt his body against hers. He wrapped his arms around her, his head resting on hers. He kissed the side of her face. "Just breathe," he whispered. "Maybe this has all been a dream."

She felt a small tear roll down her cheek and onto her pillow. *A dream.* For her, the night certainly had been.

TWENTY

JESSE

Jesse woke up the next morning surprised to find that she was still lying against him. The past night's events came back to him at once, his heartbeat picking up speed. He couldn't deny how scared and confused he was. Scared about potentially losing the only best friend he'd ever truly had, and confused about feelings he'd never dreamed he could have for her. He'd seen Quinn through her awkward teenage years, when acne and braces had caused her so much stress. They'd spent years studying together, double dating together, and complaining about their double dates later. Quinn was supposed to be the best woman at his wedding. She was supposed to be the aunt to his children. Never in a million years had he ever dreamed he could want anything else. Quinn was the one constant he'd always had—his safe spot. She kept him grounded. So, what was he going to do when she was suddenly the one making his head spin? When the feeling of her skin on his was enough to make his mind dizzy, and the scent of her on the pillow his head rested on was enough to make him contemplate missing work just to spend all day next to her?

He shook his head, trying to rid his thoughts of her. Yawning, he pulled his arm out from under her head slowly. She hardly stirred. Her hair was frazzled from sleep, her mouth hung open, and yet he couldn't help but stare at her a moment too long.

His phone chimed, causing him to jump, and he rolled over to grab it. He checked the time, cursing under his breath and climbing out of bed quickly. If he didn't leave soon, he would be late. He tiptoed across the room, grabbing his shoes and hurrying out the door. He stopped, thinking twice, and picked up a notepad from her kitchen island. He scribbled a note quickly, smiling to himself while thinking about how stereotypically 'doctor' his handwriting had become.

I'll see you tonight. I don't want it to be a dream. -J

ON HIS LUNCH BREAK, Jesse hurried to the far end of the hospital. He entered the obstetrician's office, feeling entirely out of place. The pink office was quiet, all eyes on him. He stood a few feet from the counter until a young receptionist waved him up.

"Can I help you?" she asked hesitantly.

"I need to make an appointment for a friend of mine."

She looked behind him. "Is she with you?"

"No, not yet. She just wanted me to get this taken care of."

She shook her head. "We don't really do that." She looked over her shoulder as if looking for help, but no one was there.

"Look," he said, "I know this is sort of an odd request. She's one of Doctor Turner's patients. She is nine weeks pregnant and has had no prenatal care so far." He pulled out his name badge and laid it on the counter. "I work here. I'm really just trying to help out a friend, so if you could tell me what I need to do," he said, staring at her name tag, "Sharon, I would really appreciate it."

She pursed her lips, beginning to type on her keyboard. "I'll see if there's anything I can do. What's the patient's birthdate?"

He paused. "Um, I'm sorry, I don't know that." His hand went to his head, cursing himself. He should've thought to have brought her chart. Or at least written down her information.

"I need the birthdate if you want to make an appointment, sir."

"Can't you just search her by name?"

She shook her head firmly. "I'm sorry. It's against policy."

"I work here," he told her again. "I know you can do it."

"It's against policy," she repeated a little louder. "If you want to return with the patient's birthdate, I can schedule the appointment then. Otherwise, there's nothing I can do for you." She looked like she was enjoying telling him 'no' much more than she should have.

He nodded. "Okay, fine. I'll be right back then." He turned away from the counter. There was so much he didn't know about the mysterious woman who was about to make him a father.

TWENTY-ONE

JESSE
TWO WEEKS LATER

Nova laid on the table, her knees shaking. The room around them was cold, and Jesse had been pacing for the last fifteen minutes.

"It's okay," Jesse reassured her as she shivered. "Remember, this is just an ultrasound, like the one I did before." She squeezed her hands together, biting her bottom lip and fidgeting with her clothes. Jesse moved to her quickly, taking her hands in his. "It's going to be fine. Just relax."

She looked up at him, finally making eye contact. "Thank you for coming with me today, Jesse. I know I've been shitty to you." Her dark eyes had fear plastered in them.

"You're scared," he said. "So, you get to do whatever

it takes to help you through that. I promise not to complain."

"Aren't you? Scared, I mean."

He swallowed, looking away. "Of course I am."

"You seem so sure about all of this." She smiled with one side of her mouth.

"I'm not sure about anything, except that I'm going to work my ass off for this little guy. Or girl." He reached his hand up, placing it on her belly. She surprised him by placing her own hand on his.

"Have you always wanted to be a dad?"

"Eventually, yeah. Once I was married." *Quinn.* There was her face again in his mind, her auburn hair falling into the amber eyes he could get lost in. "But, this is good, too."

She rubbed the back of her neck, looking unconvinced.

"What about you?" he asked. "You never wanted kids?" It was an in, and he had to take it.

"Well, I don't—" She took a breath as the door opened, interrupting them.

A dark haired ultrasound tech entered. "Are we ready?" she asked, a bright smile on her face.

"As we'll ever be," Nova answered.

The girl walked over, sitting down on the padded stool. "I guess you're Dad?" she said, facing Jesse.

He grinned. "That'd be me."

She nodded, turning back to the screen. He was surprised when she didn't looked phased, though he guessed that they must see it all. "When was the first date of your last menstrual period?" she asked, typing in the date as Nova answered. "And this is your first ultrasound, right?"

Nova confirmed that it was, though that technically wasn't the truth. She was protecting Jesse. She wasn't sure if there could be any repercussions for his impromptu ultrasound on her before, and though Jesse doubted it, he was thankful for her efforts.

"Okay, I'm going to have you unbutton your pants and lift your shirt up above your belly for me." She faced Novalee, gesturing toward her belly.

Nova did as she was told. Jesse, his face suddenly burning, looked away out of respect. The tech placed a pad at Nova's beltline to keep her pants clean as she smeared jelly on her lower stomach. "It may be a little cold," she warned. After a few moments, Jesse heard her voice again. "And there it is." His gaze fell to the screen, where the small white spec had somehow doubled in size since he last saw it. The lump in his throat was back.

"There's the head," she said, labeling it on the screen as she spoke, her nails clicking across the keyboard. "And there you can see a little arm." She smiled.

He looked down to Nova, who was—much to his surprise—staring at their child in awe. She looked up at him after a moment, her eyes filled with wonder.

"I can see it," she said. "I thought it would be too small."

The technician smiled at them, waiting a moment before she went on. "You're eleven weeks now, so your little guy or girl is definitely able to be seen on a scan.

There's the heartbeat." She placed a finger on the screen. "If you look closely you can see the little flutter. You probably aren't far enough along yet to hear it with the doppler but the ultrasound picks it up." She turned a knob on the computer so they could hear the *whoosh*-ing of the tiny, quick heartbeat.

Jesse's own heart jumped at the sound. He checked the screen, watching as it measured the heart rate. His eyes went back to Nova immediately, watching her watch the baby. "It's strong," he told her.

She exhaled a pent-up breath. He watched as small tears began to line her eyes. In that moment, he felt relief wash over him. *The baby was safe.* He could see the love in her eyes, though she may deny it.

She looked down at her stomach, blinking back tears. "So, it's healthy? Really?"

Before Jesse could answer, the technician spoke. "Your doctor can take a closer look at the scans with you. But I don't see anything that gives me concern."

She frowned, touching her stomach as the probe was removed. Jesse handed her a few paper towels to wipe up the jelly. When she was done, the woman handed her a roll of pictures. "I'll step out now that we're done. Your doctor will be in shortly." She patted Nova's arm as she walked out. "Congratulations, you guys."

When the door was shut and they were alone again, Nova's gaze fell to Jesse. Her fingers were caressing the black and white sonogram. "You think...I mean, I know my age is an issue, right?"

He touched her hand, wrapping his fingers around

hers. "Don't worry until there's something to worry about." He looked over the pictures with her. "The baby looks great," he whispered, trying to make her believe him. "The heartbeat is strong, it's a good size. You're doing awesome."

She ran a hand over her belly again. "I just don't want you to get too hopeful."

"Hey," he said, staring at her, "as long as you take care of yourself, that's all anyone can ask of you. The rest is out of your hands." His mouth grew dry, wanting to say so much more but finding himself unable to form the words.

The door opened and a short blonde doctor walked in. "Well, hello Novalee. It's nice to meet you. I'm Doctor Summers." She sat down, her eyes locked on Nova. "It looks like we had a healthy ultrasound, which is a great sign. So, let's talk about what comes next."

TWENTY-TWO

JESSE

They sat at his kitchen table, their takeout in front of them, but all Jesse could seem to do under the weight of the thick tension was pick through his oyster pail.

"So, what did your parents say? What was their reaction when you told them about me?"

He stuck a piece of orange chicken into his mouth, allowing a moment to come up with an answer. "They were shocked," he said finally. At least that was the truth.

"And they told you I'm horrible, right?" She twisted her mouth in thought. "Your parents were never my biggest fans."

He remained still, studying her. "I don't care what they think."

"I'm sure that's not true," she said, twirling her fork in her noodles. "You're their angel son."

"I'm no angel."

She rolled her eyes. "Somehow I doubt that. At least you were until I got my hands on you." She stared at him a moment too long. "So, tell me about the girl."

"Girl?"

"From the botanical garden. The one you introduced me to. Is she your girlfriend?"

He nearly choked on his food, coughing loudly. "No," he said, when he could catch a breath. "No, she's just a friend. Why?"

"I was just asking. I think, if we're going to do this, we should know a little bit about each other."

"That works for me."

"Does she...know about the baby?"

He nodded. "Yes, of course. I'm not hiding it. Quinn's my best friend; I tell her everything."

"Does she think we're completely crazy?"

He raised an eyebrow. "It doesn't matter to me what anyone else thinks." She rubbed her temple, leaning back in her chair. "But no, to answer your question, Quinn is nothing but supportive."

She looked up at him, staring in shock. "Am I crazy for feeling so different all of the sudden? About the baby, I mean. I still don't want to keep it, but it's like...I don't know how to explain it. I guess it feels real to me now."

"There's nothing that says you have to keep it. I told you, I'll do everything." He lowered his head, trying to catch her gaze when she looked away. "But, there's nothing that says you can't stick around, either...if you decide that's what you want. The ball's in your court here."

She smiled. "It's like you've been preparing for this moment your whole life."

"What do you mean?"

"You know all the right things to say and do."

He looked down, feeling embarrassed. It seemed like the opposite to him; he was doing everything wrong. "I'm learning right along with you, Nova."

"I'm glad it's you I'm getting to experience this with. Other men, especially men your age, might not be so nice."

Jesse swallowed. "Men like your ex-husband? Was he mean to you?" He wasn't sure if that was too personal to ask. Then again, what they were going through together was as personal as it gets.

"Travis?" she asked, waving a hand as if that were ridiculous. "Nah. He's harmless. Useless too," she said with a scoff.

"Did you two have a bad divorce?"

She ran a hand through her hair. "Not particularly bad. I mean, what divorce is good, right? But it was inevitable. Our problems were just getting worse as the years passed, and Travis never was the type to fix what was broken."

"I'm sorry," he offered.

She blinked, shrugging. "Nothing to be sorry about. Life goes on."

"You're a beautiful woman, Novalee," he told her honestly. "You deserve to be with someone who makes you happy."

"I make myself happy," she said. "I don't need anyone

else. Like it or not, we're all on our own in this world. Having someone to wake up next to doesn't change that."

"You honestly believe that?"

"I do," she said, her eyes dark. "There's so much of the world you haven't seen yet, Jesse. Things I hope you never have to see."

"Just because I'm young—younger than you—doesn't mean my life has been nothing but sunshine and roses." She'd struck a nerve, though he tried to hide it. "I've known pain and loss just like everyone else. I'm human." She took a bite of her food, chewing it slowly. "Nova, there's something I want to ask you."

She nodded, her gaze locked on the wall. "I figured it was coming."

"Have you...is this your first child?"

She rubbed her lips together, taking a deep breath. "Jesse, I know what people think of me. I know my reputation in this town. Just like I know you know the answer to that question."

"You were pregnant before," he said. It wasn't a question. She looked his way, neither confirming or denying it. "Did you—" He couldn't finish the sentence, his stomach churning at the thought.

"It was a baby girl," she said, her voice shaking. "I wanted to name her Emalee. With an 'a' and two 'e's.'" Her eyes filled with sudden tears, her hands cradling her flat stomach. "I know what your parents told you about me, Jesse. It's what anyone in Dale will tell you if you ask 'em. I was Dale's little scandal there for a while." She wiped a tear from her cheeks. "It's the worst thing I've ever done. I was a stupid, impulsive teenager with a temper out of this world. And I let a man get the best of me. I promised myself after that night that would never happen again. Until along came Travis. Which is why I'm adamantly against changing my life for anyone else. No matter how small." She touched her belly, lowering her head in defeat.

"So, it's true then?" he asked, the weight of her confession taking his breath away. Deep down, he'd refused to believe it could be true. It was just too horrible. He looked up, trying to decide what to say next.

Just then, a knock sounded at the door and he heard Quinn's voice echo through the house. "Jesse?"

Nova stood from the table, wiping her tears away quickly as Quinn appeared.

"Oh, I'm sorry," she said, seeing Nova. "I'm interrupting." She looked disappointed. "I'll come back."

Nova stepped forward. "No, I should be going anyway. You can stay."

"Don't go," Jesse said, not sure who he was talking to. Nova hurried past Quinn, who watched with wide eyes. "Nova, wait," he called half-heartedly. What else was there to say? He needed to get his thoughts together before speaking to her again. What she'd confessed to wasn't easy to process.

When the front door slammed, Quinn winced. "I'm sorry. I didn't know she'd be here. I just figured the car outside was from one of your neighbor's friends again."

"It's okay, you didn't do anything wrong."

"Do you want me to leave? You can probably still catch her."

He shook his head. "Don't worry, we both needed a minute." He lowered his brow. "What are you doing here anyway?"

She grinned, clasping her hands in front of her and rocking on the balls of her feet. "You're off for the next two days, right?"

He grabbed their food, clearing it from the table. "Yeah, why?"

"And you aren't on-call?"

"Not that I've been told."

"Good," she said, "pack a bag, then. I've got surprise for you." She held her keys in the air, wiggling them.

"A surprise? What are you talking about?"

"We are crossing an item off your bucket list."

"I don't know, Quinn. I've got a lot on my mind. Now might not be the best time," he admitted.

"Which is exactly why we're going. Trust me, Jesse, you need this. Come on, I'm begging." She puckered her lip, holding her hands up in prayer.

He threw the food in the garbage, approaching her. "What are you up to, crazy girl?"

She twitched her nose. "You'll just have to wait and see."

TWENTY-THREE

QUINN

They arrived in Key West a little over five hours later, the air around them hot and sticky. Quinn led him out of the airport, hopping into a waiting cab.

"Okay, I still don't get it," he said as they approached the hotel. "What bucket list item are we crossing off? We've been to Florida a hundred times."

She looked at him in disbelief. "You really don't remember?" He shook his head. "We were twelve or thirteen and we came here for summer vacation. You told me there was one thing you *had* to do before you got, and I quote, 'old and lame.' I figure having a kid is as close as you'll ever get to that." The excitement was nearly too much for her as she begged him silently to remember.

Suddenly, his eyes lit up. "You're not serious."

She nodded, a small squeal escaping her throat. "Dead."

"You're taking me shark diving?" His face was almost childlike.

"I sure am." She was proud of herself. "You're going to be a dad soon, Jess. A real, live, walking, talking kid is going to be relying on you for, like, *everything*. This is your last chance to be young and free." He stared at her, his eyes full of wonder, and she couldn't help but be curious what he was thinking. "What? Bad idea? Have you outgrown your shark obsession?" She winced. He'd been so young when he'd confessed this goal to her, after all. So much had changed since then.

"No," he answered. "No, it's..." He seemed to be lost in thought. "It's exactly what I need right now, honestly."

"Really?" She clasped her hands in front of her chest. "I'm so glad."

The cab came to a stop in front of the hotel and they climbed out, heading to the trunk for their luggage. Jesse made a move for his wallet to pay the waiting driver but Quinn was faster.

"This trip is on me," she told him. "So, enjoy it while it lasts."

The reservations were already made, so Quinn was able to get them checked in pretty quickly, taking two keys from the front desk attendant's hand with a grin. She led him to the elevator, both bags in his hands. When they climbed on, he watched her face light up as the elevator lurched. She'd always loved riding in them, and he made no effort to hide how hilarious he found it.

When they made it into their room, a top floor like he preferred, she flopped on the bed and let out a sigh. The giant window overlooked the ocean and Jesse walked to it, looking out.

He took a deep breath, setting their bags down. "This is...Quinn, this is great. You must've spent a fortune," he said, looking around. "Really, this is too much."

"Well, if I'm being honest, it's not completely self-less." She pressed her lips together until they wrinkled.

"What do you mean?"

"I mean...well, obviously, it's Florida in the dead of winter, so, you know, much better than Georgia. And, also, my dad's back in town and he's staying at my house. I just...I couldn't be there, you know?" She didn't like feeling so vulnerable, even with Jesse.

"He's back?" Jesse asked, his eyes wide. "What? When did that happen?"

"Yesterday," she said, walking to the window with him and running her hand over the glass. "He's just in town for a few days, but he doesn't want to face Mom. I'm half tempted to kick him out, but honestly it's not worth the drama."

"I'm so sorry, Quinn." He sat down on the bed, looking defeated.

"It's fine. I'd just rather not think about it. I know things have been awkward between us, and we never really had the chance to talk about what happened—"

"Quinn, I—"

"Which is *fine*. Seriously, it's better. No need to discuss anything. I don't really even want to. But, I needed to be with my best friend, you know? I just needed to be with you and not with my dad. No pressure or stress."

He ran his hands over his thighs. "You've got it," he told her.

She sank into the bed next to him, patting his knee. "Now, we don't get to see the sharks until tomorrow. What do you say we spend the rest of our evening on the beach?"

TWENTY-FOUR

JESSE

Half an hour later, they had both changed into their swimming suits—Jesse in floral, orange trunks, and Quinn in a red bikini that Jesse was having a hard time ignoring. She threw a white see-through cover over her shoulders, tossing a sunhat and glasses on her head.

"Ready?" she asked, holding the room key.

He nodded. "Just waiting on you."

She turned, heading out the door. They made it onto the elevator quickly. "I'm unreasonably excited about this," she told him once the doors had closed.

He chuckled, rubbing his hand over the top of her hat. "What else is new?"

"Meaning?" she asked, eyeing him over the top of her sunglasses, even though they were indoors. The elevator stopped in the lobby and they walked off.

"Just that you're easily excitable."

She crossed her arms in a fake pout. "Are you hating on my sunny disposition?" The double doors in the lobby opened as they approached, allowing them passage. She sucked in a loud breath. "Ah, don't you just love that smell?"

"More than just about anything," he said. Being at the beach always reminded him of Quinn, even on the very rare occasion she wasn't with him. When they were kids, their parents would plan consecutive vacations to the same location. One week Jesse and Quinn would travel with her family, and then his family would come down the next week and they'd trade off. They spent two weeks out of every summer growing tan side by side. He wondered if she remembered those days as vividly as he did.

They walked across the wooden bridge, the hot sand scalding his feet the instant it touched them. She walked in front of him, her red waves dancing in the salty, sea air. Jesse couldn't stop his eyes from drifting over her curves as they were highlighted by the setting sun. She turned around to face him, a smile plastered on her face.

"Hurry up, slowpoke," she said, wiggling a 'come here' finger at him.

He took off in a slow jog, feeling a bit like a *Baywatch* character. Their toes touched the ocean at the same time and she squealed loudly. "Man, this must be what heaven feels like," she whispered, her face turned up to the sky.

He couldn't help but want to agree as he stared at

her. When she noticed his stares, suddenly looking his way, he averted his gaze. "Yeah," he said softly. "I'd imagine heaven is just like this."

TWENTY-FIVE

JESSE

Later that night, after they'd both showered the salt water off their skin, they lay in bed. A box of pizza and case of beer sat in front of them. They'd been dancing around the subject all night. *The kiss. The talk.* It was driving Jesse crazy not knowing how she felt.

Quinn opened another beer and leaned back against the pillows. Her long legs stretched out, looking extra tan in comparison to her neon shorts. He had to keep his mind and eyes occupied, or else they'd wander to places he couldn't afford to be. Earlier, when she'd climbed into bed, reaching over him to grab a slice of pizza, her boob had accidentally brushed his arm and it'd taken all he had not to get wood right then and there. *What the hell was happening to him? To them?* Quinn was...*Quinn.* She'd never affected him this way. Like it or not, it was no longer something he could ignore. He had to find out where she stood. He needed to know if she felt the change between them, too—or if he was just completely batshit insane. *Probably the latter.*

"Quinn?" he said, closing his eyes as he said her name, bracing himself for the blow.

"Yeah?"

His heart was pounding so loud in his chest he was sure she could hear it. "I, um, you know the whole elephant in the room?" he asked.

"The great big one that won't leave us alone?" Her voice was just as cautious as his.

"You're my best friend," he stated. "You know that, right?"

"Of course."

"So then, why is it things feel different between us lately? Is it just me? I mean, that kiss...it isn't just me, is it?" He felt like a raging moron—words continually pouring out of his mouth without thought or the ability to stop them. Quinn called it 'word vomit.' He wished she'd just put him out of his misery.

She shook her head, her mouth hanging open in disbelief. "Jesse, I—"

He sighed, pinching the bridge of his nose. "It's just me. I'm sorry, forget I said anything." He leaned back, feeling a sense of hopelessness fill him.

"No." Quinn sat up straight, touching his arm. "Jess, it's not just you. Of course it's not. I told you that. It's just..."

"Just what?"

She took a breath, squinting her eyes. "Do you remember a few years ago when we went on that helicopter ride in New York? After I graduated?"

"Yes." He didn't know where she could be going with that story.

"I remember thinking how perfect the city looked from way up there. It was something from my dreams. All lit up in neat, clean little lines. It was beautiful and full of so many possibilities."

He nodded. He remembered the night well. He'd taken her there to celebrate her graduation from the nursing program. Reagan and Nora hadn't been up to it. Truth be told, Reagan was always afraid to leave Dale. But Quinn shared his love of adventure. Though she'd never come out and said it, he was fairly certain the only thing keeping her in Dale was a loyalty to her parents. At one time, the thing still keeping him there was Reagan...but he wondered now, was he staying for Quinn?

"But then," she said, interrupting his thoughts, "we got back down to the ground and the facade went away. New York's streets weren't beautiful and clean like they looked from so high up. They were littered, overcrowded, and full of broken people."

"I don't get what you're trying to say." He frowned.

She squeezed his arm, looking at him with a sadness in her eyes that scared him. "What I'm trying to say is...what if we are just like the city streets?" She leaned her head to the side. "What if we only look great from a distance? I mean, on paper, we could be amazing together. We get along better than I've ever gotten along with anyone, we know *everything* about each other, we couldn't be more compatible. Trust me, I've given it a lot of thought. What it would be like." She paused, though he could tell she wasn't done. "But, what if when we get down to it...we're just a mess? What if, even though we seem perfect from where we are now, what if we get together and destroy each other? I can't bear to lose you, Jesse. You're the only good thing I have in my life some days."

He placed his hand over hers on his arm. "You couldn't lose me. Not even if you tried."

"I know you think that, and I hope you're right, but we can't be sure."

"Of course we can, Quinn. Have you met us?" He ran a hand through her hair, cupping the side of her face. "I would never let anything ruin our friendship. You have to know that."

"But things are already changing between us."

"Change doesn't equal ruin. Of course, if we do this, our relationship will change. It's inevitable. But, it could be better than ever. And, if not, at least we tried, right?"

She bit her lip. "What if we fail? Do you really think we can remain friends after a breakup? Everyone always says that but it never works. We can't be reckless about this."

"Yes," he said, leaning back and placing his beer on

the nightstand so he could hold her head with both hands. "I do believe we could stay friends if we break up. Because I wouldn't recognize my life without you. But who says we're going to break up, anyway?"

"Well, if we don't break up...that means we'd end up, like, married." She scrunched her nose, pushing his hands away. "That's insane."

"So, what are you saying?" he asked, picking a piece of pepperoni off the pizza and popping it into his mouth. "That you won't be proposing any time soon?"

"Be serious," she said, shoving his shoulders.

"I am," he admitted, his eyes locking with hers. "I am serious about you, Quinn. About us." He held his hands up, stopping her from interrupting. "And I know...I know all of the million reasons why this might be a horrible idea."

She lowered her gaze, her dark lashes masking the eyes he'd learned to read years ago. "But, there's only one reason that should stop us from even trying—and I'm not hearing it."

She looked up at him, her lips parted slightly.

"Tell me this isn't something you want, Quinn. Tell me we won't work because you don't—can't—think of me in that way." He watched her eyes studying him, blinking rapidly. "Because if you can't, then we have to give ourselves a real shot here, right?"

"No," she whispered.

His heart fell, his throat growing tight. "No?"

"No," she said, avoiding his gaze. "No, I don't feel

that way about you." He let out a breath, trying not to show his pain. "I'm sorry, Jess, I—"

"No," he said, "you have nothing to be sorry about. I...misread, misunderstood, I guess." He wiped his forehead. "We should just go to bed."

"Please don't be mad," she begged, standing up on her knees on the comforter.

"I'm not mad," he assured her. He meant it. Emotions flooded his heart and brain, though anger was nowhere to be found. Not at her, at least. "Honestly, I'm...more embarrassed than anything."

"Don't be." She reached for his hand, his skin on fire from her touch.

"I just think I need to sleep this off. We're fine, Quinn. I swear. Besides," he added when her face fell, "we need to get plenty of rest for our big day tomorrow."

She smiled, though her heart was obviously not in it. He stood up, moving the pizza box off the bed. "Do you want the last piece?" he asked.

"No thanks," she said, her voice low. She slid the covers out from under her feet, lowering herself under the sheet.

It was different. Painfully so. Awkward. He was responsible for the change—for allowing himself to hope. He placed the pizza box beside the small trash can and stuck the remaining bottles of beer into the mini-fridge.

"Goodnight," he whispered as he slid into bed beside her, praying the tension would ease by morning. He flipped off the television, knowing Quinn couldn't fall asleep with it on, and reached up to turn off the lamp above him.

"Goodnight," she said once the room was completely dark. He rolled so he was facing away from her, bunching the covers under his chin. Normally, feeling her so close to him wouldn't be a problem, but tonight he was uncomfortably aware of her calf near his foot, her body heat under the same cover as his.

He closed his eyes, hating himself for doing this to them. How could he have possibly thought this would end any differently? *Of course* she didn't feel that way about him. Quinn loved her freedom. She always had. Quinn had seen him through the worst and most awkward times of his life—like when he got so drunk in college he tried to hit on a cardboard cutout of a drama student promoting the latest school play. Or when he'd been so sick with the stomach flu he hurled his guts up into her purse. Quinn had seen every side of him—it wasn't exactly attractive.

But then again, he'd seen those sides of her. He'd been the one plying her with gatorade and crackers through her week-long stomach virus in college. He'd let her cry on his shoulder—snotty ugly crying—more times than he could count. And, none of that made him see her any different.

The more he thought, the more the anger overtook him. Anger at himself for feeling the way he did; anger at her for not loving him back.

Wait...love? His eyes popped open. *Did he love*

Quinn? As a friend, sure, but he wasn't *in love* with her. Not yet. He couldn't be...could he? It wasn't—

"Jess?" Her voice rang out in the darkness, interrupting his thoughts.

He cleared his throat. "Umm, yeah?" She sat up, facing away from him. "Qui—" he began when she didn't speak right away, but the next words she spoke interrupted his.

"I lied."

TWENTY-SIX

QUINN

"I lied," she repeated, turning to face him. The moonlight barely illuminated traces of his face.

"You lied?"

Her heart pounded as she nodded, though she knew he couldn't see. "I said I don't think about you in that way. That was a lie."

She felt him move, his body edging closer to hers. His palms were on her cheeks, his breath on her skin. "You do feel it?" he asked. "The difference?"

She sighed. If she was going there, she was really going to go there. "Jesse, I've been in love with you for years." She felt braver with the light off. Brave enough to tell him a truth she'd never been able to before. "I've always wanted you to come around to how I feel, but when you finally did...I don't know, I just panicked." Her voice grew higher as her fear grew.

"Shhh," he said, running a hand over the back of her head. "Why wouldn't you tell me?"

"For all the reasons we've already discussed. But also because our timing was always off. One of us was always with someone else. And, you didn't see me like you are now. And I knew that. I didn't want to have feelings for you when you didn't feel the same way."

"I'm an idiot. I didn't—"

"It's just a fact, you don't have to feel bad. I was your dorky friend. The klutz who broke your soccer trophy in fifth grade, the girl you chased fireflies with, the one you came to when the latest girl you liked broke your heart. That was my role in your life, I never thought you'd see me as more. Not until the wedding. Something changed that night for you, I remember thinking it on the way to Atlanta. You were looking at me differently. And then you kissed me and I knew for sure. Somehow, someway, you were finally where I've been wanting you to be. But I've been there for years."

"Years?"

She nodded against his hands, feeling the sting of tears in her eyes. "This is everything I've wanted for so long. So, why do I suddenly feel so afraid?"

"Because it's change. It's a big change."

"Yeah, it is."

He pressed his lips to her forehead and cold chills ran down her spine. "Jesse, I—"

"Shh," he whispered again, putting a finger to her lips. She could taste the salt on his skin. "Don't think about it. Don't think at all. Turn your brain off for one night and just be here with me. Let yourself feel whatever you're feeling, no reservations. Just let me convince you."

Her skin was on fire as his hands brushed her shoulders. His mouth enveloped hers, his stubble brushing her skin. She sighed, feeling herself relax into his arms as they went around her.

He moved her hair from her face, his hands gentle. Everything seemed to move in slow motion, though the room around them spun. She felt cool tears collecting in her eyes as his tongue swiped hers.

He froze, and she knew he'd felt her tears. "Are you okay?" he asked, his breathing labored.

"I'm...perfect," she answered, knowing it was true. There had never been a more perfect moment.

His mouth was back on hers in an instant, this time more passionate than before. His hands swept over her body, respectful yet curious. He pulled her face closer to his, her hands intertwining behind his head. Their mouths didn't separate as he lifted her up and laid her down onto the bed, sliding his body on top of hers. His strong arms held him up, one elbow on the bed, one hand in her hair, and she couldn't help but run her hands over the muscled, defined shoulders he'd worked so hard for.

Her eyes rolled back in her head, feeling like she might wake up from her dream at any moment. Her pulse raced, her heart hammering in her chest as her thoughts raced. It was Jesse. She was kissing Jesse. More importantly, he was kissing her back.

She could feel the hardness in his pants as he shoved himself up against her thighs. She smiled through their kisses. No matter how many times she'd dreamed of this moment, she couldn't deny the sense that it couldn't really be happening.

She ran her hands under his shirt, her fingers swirling in the hair that covered his chest. She ran her nails down his back and he groaned, biting her bottom lip lovingly. Pulling back, their breaths hot and quick, he rubbed a hand over her arms, looking her over in the trail of moonlight that cascaded across her face.

"Are you sure this is okay?" She nodded, trying to catch her breath. "We don't have to do anything tonight, Quinn. That wasn't why I said what I said. You know this isn't about sex for me."

Relief she hadn't been expecting washed over her. She wanted him, there was no question, but it didn't feel right tonight. Not just as their feelings had been thrown out into the open. She needed time to process what everything meant. "Let's just take it slow," she said, her body pulsing for him. As usual, her head would win this war.

He let out a deep breath, lying down beside her. "Yeah, that's probably for the best." His hands rested on his chest as it rose and fell.

"Jess?"

"Yeah?"

"Slow doesn't mean we have to stop altogether," she whispered, elbowing him.

On cue, he flipped over, pulling her face to his. "Slow is good." He smiled, letting out a small laugh as their lips met again, this time slowly. His kisses came in slow motion, teasing her. "Slow is my favorite."

TWENTY-SEVEN

JESSE

Jesse woke up the next morning with a rushing heart. He rubbed his eyes, smiling up at the beauty staring at him from across the pillow. She was lying on her stomach, head propped up in one hand.

"Good morning," she whispered, her voice throaty from sleep.

"Good morning." He stretched his arms out, yawning loudly.

"Are you ready for today?" She twirled a piece of her hair between her fingers.

"I'm ready to go anywhere with you," he told her, rubbing his eyes, his vision still blurry.

She rolled her eyes playfully. "Don't get all cheesy on me, Mathis."

He sat up, stretching. "Whatever you say, Reynolds. But I can't make any promises." He reached out and took her hand, kissing her fingertips. "Last night was amazing."

"Oh, is that right?" She rested her tongue on the tip of her teeth. "That was just pregame." She winked.

"I know." He smirked. "I'm dying for round one."

She put her face in her palms, squealing. "Is this really happening?"

He kissed her forehead. "Want me to pinch you to verify?"

She stood up from the bed. "I don't need any doses of reality, thank you very much. I'm very content just living in my dream world. Now, go get your suit on and brush your teeth. We only have an hour before we have to get on the boat."

He pulled the covers off his legs, shaking his head. "Whatever you say, *Mom*."

"Okay, ew," she said, cringing. "Nope. That doesn't work anymore. You definitely can't call me 'Mom,' not even when I'm being naggy."

"Agreed," he said, disgust on his face. "Never again."

As he made his way into the bathroom, she called out again. "Today will be a day to remember, Jess." She was talking about the sharks, of course, but he knew he'd remember this day even if they never left the hotel room —*especially* if they never left the hotel room.

TWENTY-EIGHT

JESSE

"And now we wait," the guide said, shaking the salt water off his arm. Jesse watched the blood and guts the man had called 'chum slick' as it danced around in the water. It smelled like pure death.

"How long does it take?" Quinn asked, shifting her weight from one foot to the other. *She was nervous.*

"Could be ten minutes, could be an hour," the man said. "Just keep your eyes peeled." He flipped his shoulder-length brown hair over his shoulder, causing Jesse to scowl. The guide, his tanned body glistening in the sun like a pumped up sunscreen commercial, hadn't made an effort to hide his attempts to flirt with Quinn.

"So, what brings you two out here?" he asked. "Honeymoon? Anniversary?"

"No," Quinn answered, a little too quickly for Jesse's taste. Her eyes darted to meet his. Both men stared at her, waiting for a response. "We're just here to cross this off our bucket list."

"Ah, I see," the guide said, taking a step closer to her. "So, are you together, then?"

Come on, Jesse thought, scoffing. He could no longer hide his disdain, though he couldn't help but wonder what he would have answered had the situation been reversed. What were they exactly? What did last night mean for their relationship?

He knew what he wanted the answer to be—that Quinn was his and only his—but they hadn't had a chance to discuss it. Frankly, he wasn't sure he wanted to.

Before she could answer, something caught Jesse's eye. "Look!" he called out, pointing across the water. "Is that one?"

The guide placed his foot on the raised edge of the boat, placing a flat hand on his forehead to shield his eyes. "Good eye! If you look close, you can see a few more coming up too." He leaned over, sliding the cage door back. "All right, it's time, then. You guys are free to come and go into the cage as you please. They'll stick around for a while. As long as you stay inside the cage, you're completely safe."

Jesse walked to the side of the boat, looking down. He could see the herd circling the boat. "They're incredible," he said in awe. He reached out for her, pulling her to his side. His arm went around her waist and she leaned into him, her face lighting up as she looked down into the water.

"Holy crap," she exclaimed, making him laugh. "They're huge."

"What were you expecting?"

"Not that," she said, biting her lip. "They're amazing."

"Are you ready?"

She nodded, grabbing their snorkels and goggles from the guide. They slipped them over their heads, and Quinn immediately let out a loud laugh. "Oh, god. Not your best look."

"Well you should see yourself," Jesse retorted, making a face.

"Thank you for not allowing us to bring phones," Quinn said to the guide, sticking out her tongue at Jesse. "You first."

Jesse approached the cage, throwing a leg over the side of the boat. The water was surprisingly cold and his teeth began to chatter both from the temperature and adrenaline. Without giving himself a chance to reconsider, he pushed off the side of the boat and into the white metal cage.

The water collided with his face, fanning through his hair as he sank to the bottom. Several sharks swam under the cage and he watched them in utter fascination until he ran out of air, pushing himself back up to the surface.

"You've got to get in here," he told Quinn, holding his arm out for her. "It's crazy...they're so close."

She climbed over the side of the boat. "I'm coming, I'm coming. I was just making sure you didn't get attacked first."

"Gee, thanks." He held on to the top of the cage, taking her hand and helping her slide in. She put her weight on him, leaning over and peering into the water with her goggles. He went under, swimming to the bottom and waving for her to come down. She filled her cheeks with air, following his lead. Despite his fascination with their surroundings, he was finding it increasingly difficult to take his eyes off of her. Her face lit up wildly, both hands on the white metal bars that surrounded them as the sharks circled, paying them no mind.

After a moment, Jesse pulled her back to the top, growing desperate for air.

"This...is...amazing," she said, pushing her hair back as small tendrils had begun escaping the strap of her goggles. "Thank god for twelve-year-old Jesse."

"Yeah," he agreed. "Thank god for twelve-year-old us."

She smiled. "We were pretty great, weren't we?"

"Were...are...will be," he promised. And then, without conscious preparation, he was kissing her. In the light of day, in front of the guides and the sharks, he was kissing his best friend—because at that moment, he wanted the entire world, Quinn included, to know she was his.

TWENTY-NINE

JESSE

At the restaurant later that evening, Jesse was finding it nearly impossible to keep his hands off his date. She ran her fingers over his on the tabletop. "Back to the real world tomorrow," she said with a sigh.

He nodded. "Unfortunately."

"Do you miss the hospital when you aren't there? I know sometimes I get stir crazy without something to keep me busy. It's like, sometimes I think I'd rather live there than have to go home. Don't tell Tedlock," she added with a laugh. "She'd probably take me up on that."

"Probably," he said, joining in the laughter. "Normally, yes, I miss it when I'm away," he said, "but to be honest, I haven't thought about it once since we've been here. You keep me distracted."

She blushed, lowering her gaze. "When we go back...are we leaving all of *this* here?"

"All of what? Us?" he asked, confused.

"Mhm."

He turned his hand over, clasping hers. "I don't want that. This wasn't just some fantasy excursion while we were away from home for me, Quinn."

"So, what then? You want to...*date?*" She raised an eyebrow.

"For lack of a better term, yes." He studied her. "You don't?"

"It just seems so...small compared to what we are. I mean, we practically spend every spare moment together anyway. What will be different?"

He smirked, rubbing a hand over his mouth. "Well..."

"Besides the obvious, perv." She blushed.

"Nothing." He stared at her for a moment before leaning forward to continue. "Isn't that what's great? We've been dating all this time. Now it's just the feelings that are different. Nothing else has to change."

"And what are those feelings, exactly?"

Jesse touched her cheek with his free hand. "I'm...I'm in love with you, Q."

She reeled back, panic filling her eyes. "Are you sure? It's not just the atmosphere? The excitement of being in a new place? The alcohol?" She ran a finger over his glass. "I mean, you're having a baby with another woman. A woman you hardly know. Your feelings must be all over the place. I'm just trying to protect your heart here, Jess." She paused. "And my own."

He stood up, moving to the seat beside her so he could lower his voice further. He leaned over his knees, looking into her soft amber eyes over the freckles that covered her cheeks. "My life is a mess right now, you're right. It's a complete and total disaster. And yes, I'm going to have a baby. I don't really know what that's going to mean for me. Or for us. But, what I do know is that I want there to *be an us*. Quinn, throughout my life, through every bad thing that has ever happened to me— my knee injury in college, every breakup, when my grandma died, and now this thing with Nova—you've always been this constant white light there to let me vent or cry or scream. You've been the one good thing in my life. Always. You make me smile, and laugh; you know me better than anyone in this world. And, I don't know why it has taken me so long to fall for you, to open my eyes and see what was right in front of me all this time, but I have. And I am. And, I know now that, despite my mess of a life, you are the one I want. You. Us. This. You are the person I want to fall more in love with every single day. You're my best friend, Quinnie, but you're also the woman I'm in love with. So, no matter where my head is, my heart is with you."

Tears welled in her eyes and she looked away, blotting them quickly. "Jesse," she said when she looked back at him. "I—I'm—I love you, too." She nodded, leaning into his palm as he held it out to caress her cheek.

Just then, his phone began buzzing in his pocket. "Hold that thought," he said, pulling it out and glancing at the screen. "It's the hospital," he said. "I'm not on call, they should know that." He slid his finger across the screen, putting it to his ear. "This is Jesse."

"Jesse Mathis?" a woman's voice came across the line. He didn't recognize it.

"This is Cara, calling from St. George's Medical Center in Dakota, Georgia."

"Cara, I'm a doctor at your hospital," Jesse said, recognizing her tone and realizing this wasn't a call about his job. "What's going on?"

"We have a patient here with you listed as her emergency contact."

"Oh god," he said, his heart plummeting. "No."

"What is it?" Quinn asked, seeing his face.

"The patient's name is Novalee Phillips. Are you familiar with her?"

"Yes," he said. "She's carrying my baby."

"You need to get down here as quickly as you can."

"Is everything all right?" he asked, though he knew she wouldn't say.

"Please just get to the hospital right away. We will explain everything when you arrive."

He hung up the phone. Quinn was already standing, her face ghost-white. "Let's go," she said, knowing.

Without a word, he led her out of the restaurant, dropping a wad of cash on the table without counting it. It would be more than enough. *Oh, Novalee, what have you done?*

THIRTY

QUINN

The flight home was spent in near silence. Jesse's pale face, dry lips, and darting eyes let her know he was completely terrified. Quinn couldn't help but blame herself for barging in and essentially running Nova off during their last encounter—though that was never her intention.

If something had happened, Quinn wasn't sure the guilt would ever leave her. What would happen to her and Jesse? They'd finally gotten to a good place, but she couldn't imagine what losing the baby would do to him. *If that was what had happened,* she reminded herself. Her foot tapped of its own accord, her nails chewed down as far as they could be without bleeding. Nope, scratch that, the pinky nail was bleeding.

Jesse hadn't let go of her hand for more than a second since their flight had taken off and she didn't dare move, though her bladder was beginning to burn. Beside her, he leaned his head back into the seat, his Adam's apple bobbing as he swallowed.

"Jess, did they tell you anything else?" she whispered, rubbing his arm with her free hand.

He shook his head, not looking her way. She let out a breath of air, wishing there was something she could do to ease his mind. There was nothing. In fact, this whole situation was so completely out of her control, and that was killing her. Quinn was a woman who loved control. She liked facts, logic, sensibility. Nothing in her life felt like she could control it anymore, and she wasn't sure she'd ever feel okay with that. Only a little more than three hours ago, she wasn't sure anything could be done to spoil this evening for her. And then, the universe laughed.

She closed her eyes, resting her head against the seat as well, trying to clear her mind for just a second. She was no use to Jesse in this petrified state, but she couldn't seem to calm down. At least she could make sure to not let him see her panic. She was good at that. She let out a breath, opening her eyes and offering him a reassuring smile. He smiled back though his eyes weren't in it, his gaze glossy.

Overhead, the pilot came on the speaker to let them know they'd be landing soon and to expect a bit of turbulence. She had to actively try not to scoff at his words. *Turbulence*—yeah, that was the story of her life lately.

THIRTY-ONE

JESSE

When they arrived at the hospital, Jesse's entire body was on edge. His head pounded as he raced through the doors. Quinn followed him, dragging both their suitcases. He hadn't spoken to her much on the flight home, his voice seeming to be lost. Every time he opened his mouth, cool tears filled his eyes, and so he remained silent.

"Go on," she assured him when he made a move to grab the bags that must weigh as much as she did. He didn't have time to argue. They dashed into the emergency room, approaching the counter without waiting to be called forward.

"Novalee Phillips' room," he demanded.

The nurse, looking irritated until she looked up and recognized him, immediately typed something into her computer. She nodded, her eyes focused on the screen.

"Mathis, I didn't realize you were here tonight." A

voice rang out from behind him. He turned around to see Doctor Carter staring at him, a bright white smile plastered on her red lips.

"Oh, um, no, I'm not. I'm sorry, I really can't talk. I'm here to see someone."

"Oh, I'm so sorry to hear that," she said softly.

"She's in room four-thirty with Doctor Turner," the nurse told him. Jesse patted the counter and hurried past Doctor Carter with a soft smile. Quinn was right behind him, her heels clicking on the linoleum. When they arrived in front of her door, he turned to face Quinn. He wasn't sure how to ask her to give him a moment.

"I'll wait here," she whispered, reading his face.

He took hold of her shoulders, kissing her forehead. If he wasn't in such shock, he would've told her how perfect he found her. Instead he said, "I'll be right back." He wanted to thank her for all that she'd done to keep him calm, but couldn't conjure up the words. His fist met the wood of the door with a firm knock and he pushed it open without waiting for an okay.

Nova was lying on the bed, her dark hair fanning around her head against the white pillow case. Her eyes fluttered open as he made his way to her.

"Hey," he said, his voice wavering as he spoke.

"Hey," she whispered, trying to push herself up from the bed. She was dressed in a white paper gown, an IV running into her hand. Fluids. No medicine, that was a good thing. He checked her machines quickly, relieved to see that everything looked normal.

"What—uh—what happened?" he asked stiffly, still deciding whether he should be mad.

"I don't know," she said, placing a hand on her stomach.

"You don't know? Is it the baby? Did you try to hurt the baby?" Anger bubbled out of him as his worst fear was spoken.

"Of course not," she said, her voice defensive. "I told you I wouldn't."

"Then what happened? Is it okay? Are you okay?"

She shook her head. "I don't know, Jesse. I think we're both okay. They really haven't told me anything. I started bleeding at home and I came here. I asked them to call you because I thought you'd want to be here. I didn't realize it would take you so long."

"I was...out of town," he said, suddenly feeling guilty for his vacation.

"Out of town? I'm sorry, I didn't realize that. I hope I didn't ruin a good time." She said it with an attitude that he chose to ignore.

"Don't be sorry, I'm glad you called. You were right, I do want to be here. What did they tell you?"

"Nothing yet," she said with a softer tone. "They did an ultrasound, and Doctor Turner said he wanted to run more tests. But that was hours ago, and I've only seen nurses since. They won't tell me—" She stopped, tears filling her eyes as she spoke. "I don't know anything else."

"Unacceptable," he muttered. "I'm going to get us some answers." He darted through the door. Quinn stood when she saw him but didn't try to stop him as he rushed past with a finger in the air. He ran through the hall, passing the elevator and hurrying to the nurses' station.

"I need Doctor Turner."

"Is everything all right?" the nurse asked.

"I need Doctor Turner in room four-thirty right now. Please."

She nodded, picking up the phone, her face slightly sour. When Jesse made it back up to the room, he paced silently, Nova's eyes following him until Doctor Turner appeared.

"What's going on?" he asked, his face worried. "Is everything all right?"

"You tell us," Jesse demanded. "This patient hasn't been informed of her medical condition. You haven't told her if our child is even still alive."

"Mathis, calm down," Doctor Turner told him, his tone irritated. "I wanted to run every test before I gave an answer I wasn't sure about. The child is fine, for now, but I wanted to figure out what could be causing the bleeding. Now, I know you're both worried, but calling me away from other patients won't fix anything until I have her lab results back."

"Lab results?"

"We ran a blood panel. I want to check a few things. It could be as simple as an infection, something we can cure with antibiotics."

"What do you *think* it is?"

The doctor sighed. "Ms. Phillips, with your last pregnancy, you told me it ended in a miscarriage, correct?"

Nova nodded.

He scratched his head. "Was there a reason your doctors removed the fetus via cesarean?"

"They did what?" Jesse demanded, thinking back to her first ultrasound. Had he noticed the small silver scar that would indicate a cesarean? He couldn't remember.

"I'm worried her scar could have built up tissue, which could have affected her implantation. It's all just theory at this point." He spoke directly to Jesse.

"You had a c-section?" Jesse asked, looking at Nova.

"They said it had to be done. I wouldn't have survived labor. I had lost too much blood that night," she said sadly.

"Excuse me?" both doctors demanded at once.

"After I lost the baby, they had to remove her. I was still unconscious from losing all the blood I had. They did a c-section to take her out." She looked back and forth between them. "Why are you both looking at me like that?"

"It's just very unusual that they would end a miscarriage with a c-section. Not unheard of but rare, nonetheless," Doctor Turner said plainly. "Did they give you a reason for your hemorrhage?"

"My doctor did, but it was my fault. I can promise you that isn't the reason this time. I'd rather not talk about it, if that's okay."

Turner cast a look a Jesse that said what they both knew. "I'm afraid that's not the best answer, Ms. Phillips. I need to know the reason if you want me to do everything in my power to protect your child." She looked down, not answering. After a few moments, Turner spoke up. "I'm going to leave you two alone. I'll see if I can put a rush on those results. In the meantime, she needs to rest. If you can get a medical release signed for her records, I'll send out for them. They might be what it takes to save your child." He looked him square in the eye, his wrinkled hands on the door.

Jesse agreed. Once the door was shut and they were alone once again, he face Nova. "Why wouldn't you tell him the truth?"

"Excuse me?"

"Nova, you know I know what you did and he needs to know too. He's the one trying to save our child."

"So, then tell him, why don't you? Do you think it's easy for me to just...just relive the awful things I did?" She was shaking, her face growing red. "I can't, Jesse, I just can't talk about it. Certainly not to him. Not to anyone who's going to look at me like you do when you bring it up."

"I can't tell him. I don't even know everything, but he should. And, I don't mean to look at you any certain way, Nova. I'm just scared, okay? I'm terrified that something terrible is going to happen to this baby, and I don't know if I can handle that. I'll do whatever it takes to make sure that doesn't happen." He paused. "How did you do it?"

"Do what?" She was trying to control her tears though he could see them as they fell.

"The abortion. How did you cause your abortion? You called it a miscarriage, and I let you have that little falsehood before, but if you won't tell him, I need to. Because it may be causing this child harm now. And that's not a judgement, I just want to know how. Maybe it will help me understand why such drastic measures were taken. *If* what you're saying is even true."

She pressed her lips together, closing her eyes.

"I need to know," he went on. "I wasn't going to ask, because maybe it isn't any of my business, but now...now it's affecting my child. That makes it my business, Nova. Because I love this baby—and I actually care what happens to it."

"What is that supposed to mean?" she spat at him, her voice icy.

"I know you don't care what happens to this kid, but I do. So, if you're going to lie to us and let it end up dead anyway, I need to know that in advance. Before I put my heart into this any more than it already is."

"Oh, screw you, Jesse," she bellowed. "Get out of my room!"

"No, I'm not leaving until I know what's going on."

"Get the hell out!" She threw a pillow at him, fuming. "I'm doing you a favor here, remember? Not the other way around. If I'm so horrible, then you can just get out of my room. I'll leave the baby here for you when the time comes. God forbid you even have to associate with such a miserable excuse for a person." Her voice broke, her hard outer shell finally splitting open.

He stood still, contemplating his next move. She wiped her tears as quickly as they fell, curling her arms around herself. "Look," he said, "I don't think you're a bad person, Nova. I'm just scared."

"*You're* scared? Don't you think I'm scared? The last

time I was pregnant I woke up in a hospital with no memory of how I got there. My insides felt like they were going to fall out every time I moved, and I received the news that my baby—a baby that I wanted—had died. That I had killed her. And I couldn't even remember doing it. I *wanted* her, Jesse. I never even got to see her. She was just...gone. So, yeah, when I found out I was pregnant again, I panicked. I didn't want to have this baby because it's a reminder of all that I've lost."

He was shocked at her confession. "Nova, I—" He didn't know what to say. His heart hurt as he watched her cry, feeling guilty for his harsh words. "I'm sorry."

"You don't have to be sorry. Just don't hate me for making a decision you could never understand."

He walked to her bedside, taking her hand. "I'm sorry for your loss, Nova. I'm sorry that happened to you. And I'm going to do everything in my power to make sure it doesn't happen again."

THIRTY-TWO

JESSE

Jesse walked into the hallway and found Quinn instantly. She stood up, approaching him.

"What is it?" she asked, worry filling her tired eyes. "Is the baby okay?"

"I don't know," he said honestly. "We haven't lost it yet, but the doctors are running more tests now. Turner asked her about a c-section."

"It's way too soon for that!" Quinn exclaimed.

"No, from before. She's had one in the past that they were apparently unaware of."

"What? So, does she have built-up scar tissue? It could cause a hemorrhage."

"That's what I'm afraid of," he said. "She's not far enough along for the baby to stand a chance if she has to deliver. Not even close."

"Okay, what do you want to do? We could see about

getting a specialist from Atlanta. I can make some calls." She began to reach for her cellphone.

He shook his head. "Maybe. Right now I need a copy of her records. Do you think you could get them for me? I need to find out what happened the night of her surgery. Turner asked for a release for them, but he must not realize the delivery happened here. Mom said Doctor Norwood did the surgery, so her records will be in the system. Nova doesn't want him to see them, for fear that he'll judge her, I guess, so when you do find them, just bring them straight to me. Oh, and search under 'Nova' and 'Novalee.' I'm not sure which it will be."

"Of course," she said. "I'll see what I can find."

"Thanks." He squeezed her hand before turning and walking back into Nova's room. He picked up the pillow she'd thrown at him and sat down in the chair beside her bed.

She stared at him strangely. "Thank you for being here," she said after a moment.

"Of course." He leaned forward, resting his elbows on his knees. "We're going to get this all sorted out. You're going to be okay. Both of you."

It was the one promise doctors weren't allowed to make; the one promise he couldn't afford not to keep.

THIRTY-THREE

QUINN

Quinn threw on her scrubs, tying her hair up with the ponytail holder she always kept on her wrist. Once she was dressed, she walked out the door toward the nurses' station. She was scheduled to be at work in just under five hours anyway, she may as well stay.

"Quinn, hey," Scarlett greeted her. "You've been here all night? How did I miss you?"

"Yes, but no. I've been here but not working."

She shrugged. "Well, I'm glad you're here now. Alora's been running particularly slow tonight. We could use the extra hands."

"Yeah, sure," she said. "First, I need to grab a patient's files for Turner."

"Okay," Scarlett said, grabbing the phone as it rang. "Nurses' station."

Quinn squeezed around her, logging onto the

computer. She typed Novalee's name into the search field. *Nova Phillips.* She stared at the blank screen, letting her know there were no matches. Next, she searched *Novalee Phillips.* As the record pulled up, she clicked on it, reading through the file quickly. She couldn't help the gasp that escaped her throat as she made it to the end.

"What's up?" Scarlett asked, now off the phone. Quinn hit the button to send the file to the printer, closing out of the page and moving to grab it before Scarlett could see. She picked up the stack of charts waiting for her as she headed up the hall.

"Nothing," she called over her shoulder. "I'll catch you later." Her heart pounded as she made her way to Nova's room, her hands shaking. She knocked on the door, popping her head in after a moment of no response.

Nova smiled at her stiffly, nodding toward Jesse who was asleep in the chair next to her. "He's out," she whispered.

"Oh," Quinn said, walking into the room.

"You can probably wake him up if you need to. He only just dozed off."

Quinn stared down at him, his face blissfully unaware of anything bad in the world. She felt a small smile creep onto her lips.

"I'd offer to leave, but..." Nova trailed off, holding her arm up to show an IV running into her hand.

"No, of course not. That's okay," Quinn said quickly. "But I do need to wake him. I need to get to work, but I have to talk to him about something first. It's important."

"Is it about me?" Nova asked.

"No," Quinn lied.

"Oh," she said. "I was hoping you had news about the baby."

"Not yet," Quinn told her. "I'm sorry."

"Are you? Because if I were you, I wouldn't be." Her expression was stern.

Quinn cocked her head to the side. "What do you mean?"

"You can't be thrilled about the boy you love having a baby with someone who's not you."

Out of habit, she began to deny her feelings. "I don't —" She stopped, realizing she could finally be honest. "I don't wish anything bad on you or your baby, Novalee. I'm a nurse to my core, I could never wish harm on anyone." It was true, healing was in her nature, same as it was Jesse's. "But, also, I know that to lose either of you would devastate Jesse. I'm not sure either of us could survive that."

"You'd rather be hurt yourself?"

She didn't have to think about it. "In a heartbeat."

"He told me the two of you aren't together," Nova said thoughtfully.

"We, um, actually, I don't know what we are, truth be told. And I'm not really sure he does either." She wasn't sure why she was spilling her guts out to a stranger. "He's my best friend. Always has been."

"I don't want to complicate things for you, Quinn. Either of you. But Jesse is a really special guy." She smiled at him. "And when our baby gets here—well, emotions will be running high. I won't make any apologies for what happens at that time."

"Meaning what?" She leaned her weight on the opposite foot, feeling slighted by her comments. Her body tensed as she waited for an answer that took entirely too long.

"I'm just giving you fair warning. Woman to woman. Our connection is special because of this baby. I'm not trying to hurt you, I just want you to be prepared in the off-chance he chooses me."

Quinn felt her temperature rising, realizing what Nova was saying. "Chooses you? He said you didn't want to be in this baby's life." Had he lied to her? "Now you want him to choose you? As in, be with you?"

"Six months gives me time to change my mind," she said simply. "I'm not saying I will, but I can't say I won't. My feelings for him are growing and changing as much as this child is. If I decide to stay in my baby's life, I want to give it a family. A real family. My guess is Jesse will want the same."

Venom boiled in her blood. She clenched her fists, trying to keep her face still. "You can't just...just *toy* with his feelings like that, Novalee. You need to make up your mind before you hurt him. Jesse is too good of a guy to be strung along." Anger coursed through her, her body shaking. As her voice rose, Jesse began to stir. He opened his eyes before either of them spoke again. He looked up at Quinn, smiling, and taking a moment to realize where he was. His gaze shot back and forth between Quinn and Nova before he spoke. "What's going on?"

Quinn tried to keep her voice calm. "Can I talk to you? Out in the hall?"

"Of course," he said, standing up from his chair. "I'll be back," he told Nova, brushing his hand over her arm.

She nodded, her dark eyes locking with Quinn's. When they made it out into the hall, Jesse spoke first. "Everything okay?"

"I found Nova's records for you," she said, staring at him uneasily.

"Great," he said, taking the page when she held it out. She watched his eyes dancing across it, taking in the information. When he finished, he looked at her, his eyes narrowing. "Where's the rest?"

She shook her head. "That's it, Jess. All we have on Novalee Phillips is on that page. According to our records, Nova's first visit to our hospital was just weeks ago, when she came in to have an abortion. Before that, we have nothing. That's why Turner wanted to send out for her records. We have no record Novalee even existed before that appointment. Not here anyway."

"But that means—"

"Novalee's surgery your mom told us about...it never happened."

THIRTY-FOUR

JESSE

Jesse barged into his parents' house at just past six in the morning. His father was kicked back at the table, a steaming mug of coffee and yesterday's paper in front of him.

"Jesse? What the hell are you doing here? Is everything all right?" Big Jim shot up at the sight of his son, fear filling his face.

"I need to know everything about Novalee Phillips. I need to know how she lost her baby."

His face went stony. "Who told you?"

"Mom did. And Novalee confirmed. But, their stories don't add up. Novalee said she had a c-section. Is that true?"

His father scratched his head. "Your mother should have never told you anything. We don't know what happened that night, it was all rumors and hearsay."

"Mom seemed to know quite a bit."

"How would she? Neither of us were there."

"You have your hands in everything that goes on in and around Dale, Dad. Don't try to fool me. I have a right to know. Is Novalee lying to me?"

"I told you Novalee was bad news from the get-go. You should have just listened to me. You always think you know better. That's the trouble with you millenials, no one can tell you nothing."

Jesse felt the bitterness rising in him as his father danced around the subject. "Are you going to tell me what you know, or not?"

"What I *know*," his father said, jabbing his forefinger into the table, "is that Novalee was never anything but trouble. Trash family raising nothing but trash. And then one night, she went into an alley, high as a damn kite, and she shoved a knife so far up between her legs she lacerated her cervix. And, she didn't stop there, no. She kept digging. Fucking psychopath if you ask me." Big Jim's eyes bulged with anger. "I never wanted to be the one to tell you that, Jess. But, you'll never see that baby alive. Not if you have to count on Novalee. It's a wonder she can even get pregnant as destroyed as she must be. Only stopped when she had lost so much blood she couldn't stay conscious."

Jesse sat down, the image of Nova slicing herself open filling his mind. The blood rushed from his head and he found himself unable to look his father in the eye.

"We've all gotten in a little trouble now and again, son," Big Jim continued, putting a firm hand on Jesse's shoulder. "But don't let this girl ruin your life. Your mother and I worked too hard to give you a good one."

"How do you know all of that? About Nova? How do you know it's even true?"

"Greg and Marcus." *Doctor Norwood and Doctor Reynolds.* "They were residents then, like you. They worked with your grandfather on her surgery. I don't think they've been the same since...something like that, well, you don't soon forget it."

"Grandpa? I thought he didn't do surgery."

"On the rare occasion, he did. One of the perks of running a hospital, Jess, you can do what you want."

Jesse looked down. He knew his family had a stake in the hospital somewhere down the line, and that his grandfather had been the CEO for a few years, but it was hardly brought up. His grandfather had passed away when Jesse was just under four, and his father didn't talk about him very often. Their relationship had been strained, from what Jesse could tell, though he had very few actual memories of the man.

"So, why did they do a c-section? It doesn't make any sense. She would've just lost more blood that way."

"How should I know? You'll have to check her records for that."

Jesse closed his hands into a fist. "I've already tried that. She had no records."

His father's face went grim, though no surprise resonated on the wrinkles. "Oh."

"Oh? Meaning what?"

"I don't know for sure, son, but her records may have been sealed by the legal department."

"What? What are you talking about?"

"I don't know. I know there for a while, after her surgery, she tried to sue the hospital. My father never told me the whole story, I just know what I overheard here and there. Greg and Marcus weren't involved in any of the legal stuff. I guess she was mad because they saved her life, but I'm not sure. Anyway, she had no case and it was settled out of court, but they may have sealed her records as a result."

"So, how would I get them?"

"Get what? Her records?"

"Yeah."

He scowled, rubbing his forehead. "Christ, Jesse, why do you need them? I've just told you what happened."

"I want to look them over. We're having complications with her pregnancy, but if I can figure out why, maybe we can fix it. It could all be linked to her last pregnancy. The way she lost it."

"I told you why—the woman's cervix looks like a damn tic-tac-toe board."

Jesse cringed. "Oh, real nice, Dad."

"Don't 'me-too movement' me, son. I'm just saying, she's trouble. Unstable. Abortion is one thing, I guess, but to do it that way? You won't convince me she doesn't need mental help. You can't raise a child with a woman like that, Jess."

"Even if that's all true, you don't know anything

about who she is now. It's been nearly three decades. People can change."

"They can't change that much," Big Jim said, as if he'd suggested they take a day trip to Mars.

"Do you know how I can get the records, or not?"

"No, I don't," Big Jim said stiffly. "And honestly, I don't think you need to worry yourself with them. You've heard the truth, hard as it is to hear, now it's up to you to decide what to do with it." His father stood up from the table, pulling out his wallet and sliding five one-hundred dollar bills his way. "That should be enough. Take care of this mess before it's too late."

With that, he carried his mug of coffee and newspaper out of the room, leaving Jesse alone with his thoughts.

THIRTY-FIVE

QUINN

Quinn walked into her mother's house, dropping the grocery bag onto the kitchen table with a sigh. "Mom," she called, her voice echoing through the quiet house.

In her pocket, her phone began buzzing. "Jesse," she called into the speaker. "What is it?" It had been two days since she'd heard from him.

"They're letting Nova out."

"That's great," she said. "The baby's okay?"

"Yeah, so far, so good. We just have to keep her in bed."

"We?"

"Well, me. Me and Nova."

"Oh, right. So, she'll be on bedrest then? For what...the rest of the pregnancy?"

"Possibly. We hope not, but Turner can't say just yet. We have to wait and see what happens."

Again with the *we*. A 'we' that didn't include her. "Well, I'm happy for you, Jess." Her voice was tight, clipped, but she hoped he wouldn't notice.

"Thank you," he said, then after a pause, "I miss you, Quinn."

"I miss you, too," she told him honestly.

"I know I've been distant."

"You've got a lot going on."

"Yeah," he said softly, "but that doesn't change everything I said on vacation. Things are...all around complicated right now. I know that. But, I still want to keep what we had going."

She smiled, relief hitting her. It was all that she needed to hear. "I do, too."

"Once I get everything figured out, things will settle down. And even more so after the baby's here." *After the baby's here.* Several more months. It seemed like a lifetime. "What do you mean by 'figure everything out'? About Nova's c-section?"

"Well, that and..." He paused. "I think my dad is hiding something."

"What do you mean?"

"About Nova. To protect me, I guess. He acted like he didn't know much about her past but then went on to tell me this...detailed story about the night she lost her baby."

"So?"

"So, he was very informed for someone who claimed to not know much. I don't know, Quinn. I just get this feeling there's more than what he's telling me."

"What about her records? Have you asked her about those?"

"No. I'm trying to be sensitive. I, um, well…Dad said they may have been sealed off after she threatened the hospital with legal trouble."

She gasped. "For what?"

"I don't know. He didn't seem to know, either. He said something about her trying to sue because they saved her life."

"Is that a thing?" She looked up as her mother, followed by her father, walked into the room. "Hey, Jess, I gotta go. My parents are here."

"Your parents? Both of them?"

"Yep," she said, confusion welling in her.

Before she could hang up, she heard his voice again. "Hey, actually, I need a favor. Your dad was on Nova's surgery that night. Could you ask him about it? Maybe he remembers something that could help."

"Okay. I'll see what I can do."

"I'll come over tonight."

She smiled, blush warming her cheeks. "See you then." She hung up, her eyes on her parents. "What's going on? I thought you left for Costa Rica?" she asked her father.

"Your dad is home," Shelly said testily. "For now." She stared at the groceries. "Quinnie, you didn't have to pick up my groceries."

"I was out," Quinn said, shrugging. "What does she mean you're home? Why?"

"I needed to get a few things done here. I thought

you'd be happy to see me," Marcus answered, holding out his arms for her.

Quinn grabbed the bags, helping her mother unpack them. "Are you guys, like, back together?"

"Yes," her father answered, moving his arms back to his sides.

"No," her mother said at the same time.

"We're undecided," her father said, rubbing his mustache.

"Well then," Quinn murmured, unable to think of what else could possibly be said.

"I thought you'd be happy to hear I'm back. Furthermore, I thought you'd be happy to see me *not* at your place." Her father stared at her.

She grimaced. "I told you it was no problem having you stay there."

"You did. Which is why you disappeared after just one night of having me over."

"Disappeared?" Her mother's head lifted, her gaze narrowing at her daughter.

"Oh, I didn't *disappear*. Jesse and I went to Florida for a few days. It wasn't a big deal."

"Florida, huh?" Her eyebrows shot up, a knowing look on her face.

"And it just happened that you had to go as soon as your dear old dad showed up?" Marcus put an arm around her.

"It was...a thing."

"A thing? An...*impromptu declaration of love* thing?" Shelly teased.

"No. Well," she thought aloud, "maybe." Her mother's eyes lit up. "I don't know anything yet, Mom." She had to try to talk her mom down before her excitement overflowed. "Jesse's got a lot going on right now. Speaking of," she paused, turning to face her dad. "I have a question to ask you."

"Okay," he said cautiously.

"Do you remember a patient named Novalee Phillips?"

Her father's gaze faltered. "No...I don't think that sounds familiar. Why do you ask?"

"Well, she's a few years younger than you guys, she's Big Jim's age actually, but she's...pregnant. And, it's Jesse's baby." Shelly gasped and her father took a step back, though his eyes remained locked on hers. "It's fine, though," Quinn went on. "They're working it out. The reason I asked is because she's had a c-section in the past, but it was after her miscarriage. *Because of her miscarriage.* Jesse's parents heard that she'd tried to give herself some kind of abortion, but we don't know if that's true or just a rumor. Big Jim said you were a surgeon on her case, though, so I thought...*we* thought you might be able to help us."

"I've seen a lot of patients, Quinn," he said, his jaw tight. "And you know I'm legally not allowed to discuss any of this with you anyway. What do you need exactly? Her records should be able to tell you more than I can."

"That's the problem...her records are missing. Gone. Sealed. Something. But, she's having complications with her pregnancy. Jesse's really worried. We thought having some idea of her medical history might help us figure out how to help her—if we even can."

"I'm surprised. Now that I think about it, I do think I remember having her for surgery—how could I forget something that traumatic?" He tapped his forehead. "Yep, it's in there vaguely, it seems. But, I don't remember any of the specifics." He paused. "Sorry, kiddo." He patted her hands, his eyes soft. "I really wish I could help you more."

"That's okay, I just figured I'd ask." With that, her dad stood up, walking away from her and out of the room. She turned to her mother, who had been strangely quiet. She was frozen in place, hands wound tightly around a pickle jar. "Mom?"

Her mother snapped out of her apparent trance. "Sorry, what?"

"Is everything okay?" she asked, smirking.

"Of course, baby," she replied, her mouth stiff.

"Mom, what is it?" Everything was obviously not okay.

She shook her head, closing her eyes. "I remember Novalee." Her voice was so low Quinn wasn't sure she'd heard her at first.

"From school?"

She nodded, keeping her voice low. "She was...troubled. In and out of foster care, parents both junkies. But, she was always kind. To me, at least. The way I heard it, after she lost that baby, the men in our town ran her out like a stray dog. And away she went."

"Why wouldn't Dad remember her, then? If not from

the surgery, he should remember her from school, right? Big Jim said—"

She shook her head. "All I'm going to say, Quinnie, is that I wouldn't trust Jim Mathis any further than I could throw him." She turned around, opening her fridge and placing the pickles into it. "And, for the record, that isn't far. The man's been going back for seconds way too long."

THIRTY-SIX

QUINN

That night, Jesse knocked on her door at half-past seven. She opened it quickly. It felt like it had been years since she'd seen his face, and her skin flushed as their eyes locked on each other's.

Without saying a word, he leaned in, kissing her. "I've missed you."

She shut the door behind him as he entered. "I've missed you, too." He walked past her into the kitchen and she noticed the grocery bag in his arms. "No pizza tonight?"

"Nope," he said, setting the bag down on the island. "You told me once that pizza and beer were our go-to for when we're sad. When something's gone wrong. But tonight, nothing has gone wrong. Nothing is sad. In fact, tonight is all about happiness."

"Happiness, hm?" she asked, feeling skeptical.

"Yours. Mine." He walked up to her, wrapping his arms around her waist. "Ours."

"You're in an exceptionally good mood, sir." She touched his nose with her forefinger.

He smiled, kissing her quickly before walking back to the counter. "This is everything I've been waiting on, Quinn. *You* are everything I've been waiting on. Things have been so complicated lately, with everything except you."

"So, you want me because I'm easy?" she asked with a smirk, popping open a bottle of wine.

He winked at her. "You know me all too well."

She poured them two glasses while Jesse washed his hands. "So, what are you fixing me?"

He pulled out two pints of ice cream: rocky road for her and mint chocolate chip for him. She squealed as he grabbed a bottle of chocolate syrup, chocolate chips, and caramel from the bag.

"You brought ice cream for dinner?" She watched as he pulled out the final two items from the bag: a jar of cherries—her favorite, and a bag of peanuts—his.

"What is a happier meal than ice cream?" he asked indignantly. "I challenge you to name one."

She shook her head, smiling brightly. "I don't think I can."

"When we were younger, ice cream sundaes, every Sunday...that was our tradition. I always looked so forward to that. And, we haven't done it in years. I don't even remember when we stopped. But, let's face it, that's just sad. So, as of tonight, I am officially reinstating Ice Cream Sundae Sundays."

She laughed, crossing her arms. "But, it's Tuesday."

He looked up as if he were calculating the day in his head before waving his hand. "Details." He shrugged.

She climbed up onto the barstool beside the island and took the bowl he handed her. He scooped out two perfect scoops into her bowl, laughing as she coated the mounds with chocolate syrup, chocolate chips, and two cherries. Then, he scooped one scoop of rocky road and one scoop of chocolate chip mint into his own bowl, quickly adding all of the toppings.

"All of our favorites?" she asked, raising a brow at him. She popped a cherry into her mouth, pulling the stem off.

"The perfect combination," he said, clinking his spoon to hers as if they were glasses.

She smiled. "My, my. You sure do know how to work a line, Jess Mathis." She imitated a heavy southern accent as she spoke and pretended to fan herself.

"You haven't seen anything yet, ma'am," he told her playfully, playing up his own accent.

"Hey," she said, remembering something, "I talked to my dad—"

He placed a finger on her lips, removing it seconds before his lips met hers. "Not tonight," he whispered. "We've spent so much time focused on Nova and the baby. And while I appreciate that, tonight's about you. And us."

She couldn't help but feel her cheeks heat up at his

words. His face was so close she could nearly taste the chocolate on his breath. She leaned in, pressing her cold lips to his, her heart speeding up. Her hands found his hair, her fingers running through it cautiously.

Their lips separated, their noses brushing as they both smiled. When his lips touched hers again, there was a fire in their kisses that hadn't been there before. The world seemed to tilt on its axis.

He moaned under his breath, lifting her up off the bar stool and taking her to the couch. She gripped him tight, legs around his waist. He laid her down, sliding on top of her and smiling down devilishly.

"Our ice cream is going to melt, you know."

He shook his head. "I don't care. It's not Sunday anyway."

She watched his lips move, the perfect lips she'd dreamed of kissing for so long, as her heart filled with so much joy she was sure it would explode. "Well, you really must love me, then."

"I do," he said, his face surprisingly serious. She bit her lip. "I mean it, I do," he went on. "I've never felt like this with anyone, Quinn. Like...we have such a strong connection. We were so worried about our friendship, but our friendship doesn't hinder this relationship—it helps it. We've only kissed, and already I'm on fire for you. I've never been with anyone who I care about on the level that I care about you. Hell, I didn't know this level existed." He moved a piece of hair from her eyes gently. "I care about you. I have since we were five years old, running around at our families' barbeques, but the way

I'm feeling now...it's like we're two totally different people. Like, sometimes you look at me and I see the little girl who made mud pies with me and ran through the sprinkler in her underwear—the girl I've seen as my best friend for so long. But then other times, like now, I look at you and I see this incredibly smart, gorgeous, *sexy* woman. And it's hard to explain how much I love both versions of you." He kissed her shoulder, making her insides squirm.

"You think I'm sexy?" She'd been called 'quirky' before, 'cute,' 'pretty' even, but in her experience 'sexy' was reserved for busty blondes, not rusty brunettes with glasses that fell down their nose too often.

"God, Q, you're so sexy," he told her, pressing his pelvis against her and leaning closer as if to prove it. "I don't know why I'm just seeing it now." He rubbed his hands over her cheeks. "You've been right in front of me all this time. All this wasted time. And now it's like I've finally opened my eyes."

He meant every word he was saying. It was written all over his face, and Quinn couldn't help but be mesmerized. "I'm so in love with you," he went on, "I know I've already said that tonight but I'm saying it again. Ever since the night of the wedding—when I could see you for who you should've always been in my eyes, and then the night in Florida when I finally grew the balls to tell you how I was feeling, even with all the craziness in my life, you are absolutely all I can think of."

She lifted her head up, meeting his lips. He was saying the words that had been in her heart for so long.

He sank into her, his body engulfing hers. Their kisses grew passionate—then fierce. His tongue grazed hers, his hands moving from her arms to her hips, his thumbs pressing into her hip bones.

His fingertips moved across her skin, under her shirt, his hands cool on her burning skin. Her hips swayed with his, their bodies moving together despite their clothes. She reached up, unbuttoning his shirt, her hands shaking. She pulled it off, allowing him to sit up as she pulled it from his arms. His hands went to the bottom of her shirt once again, ready to remove it.

"This is okay?" he asked before making another move.

She nodded, raising her arms so he could pull the shirt over her head. He cradled her scalp, smiling down. His eyes heated up as his gaze danced across her bare skin. He kissed her chest, his tongue drawing small circles in between her breasts. He cupped them, his mouth moving to her collar bone. His kisses were slow, his tongue cool on her skin. She squirmed as he explored further down, reaching her stomach and hips, stopping only when he reached her beltline.

"Still okay?" he mumbled, his breathing growing faster.

She nodded, running her teeth over her bottom lip. He slid his hands over the metal button on her pants, unhooking it carefully. Anticipation radiated through her. She lifted her hips, helping him slide her pants over them, her face blazing. He looked her over, his gaze intense. He looked as though he were ready to tear every piece of clothing from her skin. She couldn't keep the smile from her face as he began to kiss her again. Her passion and excitement grew more severe with every kiss. Finally, he stood up, pulling a condom from his pocket.

"You came prepared?" she asked, raising an eyebrow and pushing her glasses up on her nose.

"You can never be too prepared, Quinn," he joked. "We're really going to do this?"

She nodded, her teeth on her lips again. "Oh, yes."

His hands were unbuckling his pants in an instant, his eyes locked on hers. God, he was gorgeous—all ripped abs, toned shoulders, and Florida tan. He pulled his pants and boxers down to his ankles, stepping out of them, and sliding back onto the couch with her before she could look over him properly. He was nervous; they both were.

It wasn't like she'd never seen Jesse naked before— but this time was different. It was so different. Her pulse raced, her heart leaping into her throat as he took hold of her panties and nearly ripped them off. Her body was a furnace, every touch like lightning shooting through her.

She closed her eyes as his hand slid between her legs, his mouth on her neck. It was crazy, she'd thought it would feel so strange, being with her best friend in a way they never had before, but as he slid inside of her, their eyes locked together, their lips bouncing off each other's, nothing had ever felt less awkward. In fact, nothing had ever felt more perfect.

He waited for a second, allowing her to adjust to the feeling of him inside of her. As he started to move, he leaned down, his arms on either side of her head, face in her hair, breath in her ear. Their bodies worked together, perfectly in sync.

"I love you," he whispered, and she felt his words in her heart, knowing how true they were and being terrified by that all at once.

"I love you, too," she said, tears in her eyes as she allowed herself to take the leap off the cliff she'd been standing on for so long. She was—heart and soul, head over heels—in love with her best friend. There was no turning back now.

THIRTY-SEVEN

JESSE

The next morning, Jesse climbed out of bed, cleaned up the melted ice cream, and discarded wine glasses from the night before. He felt ten feet tall—invincible. He was high on Quinn, and he wasn't sure he'd ever felt so good. *Who knew love could feel this way?*

He started the dishes, stopping only when he heard her quiet footsteps padding down the hall. He turned around, drying his hands and waiting to see her.

"Coffee?" she asked in a throaty voice, her eyes half-closed, hair standing in every direction.

He laughed. "It's on."

She smiled, walking toward him with her sleeves over her hands. "Good morning," she whispered, wrapping her arms around his neck.

He breathed her in, so in love with even the scent of her. "Last night was..."

"Amazing," they said at the same time. He felt it, his love for her; real as a person squeezing his heart with their bare hands. It was freeing yet debilitating all at once.

"I have to get to work," she said, interrupting his thoughts. She walked over to the counter and began filling her mug with coffee. "Will you come back over tonight?"

"Of course," he promised, turning back to the dishes.

"Hey, Jess," she said, before he could turn the water on.

"Yeah?"

"Um, about my talk with my dad..."

"Mhm?" He leaned up against the island, listening carefully. He'd almost forgotten about the outside world.

"Why do you need to know the truth so badly anyway? I mean, we both know there are medical anomalies. Any number of things could've caused them to decide a c-section was in her best interest."

"I know," he said simply. "I just...I guess I need to know if she's being honest with me. And I need to know what she did. I thought I didn't want to know, but it's driving me crazy."

"Will it matter? Will it affect your decision?"

"I don't know." He sighed, crossing his arms.

"You know you might not be able to fix this. Something might happen. I know you don't want to talk about it, neither do I. But, I don't want you to blame yourself for Nova's mistakes. Or her age. Or anything else that could go wrong."

"Quinn, I won't." He was lying and they both knew it.

"He doesn't remember her. Or the surgery. Not well, anyway," she said, running her fingers along the rim of her mug.

"Oh." Disappointment overwhelmed him. "Well, that's ok—"

"But my mom does."

"Your mom?" She wasn't looking him in the eye—that worried him. "What did she say?"

"She...she said Novalee was run out of town. She said her life was really bad, before the pregnancy. Foster care, druggie parents...the works. I got the feeling there was more that she wasn't telling me."

"That's how my dad was, too."

"Listen," she said hesitantly, "about your dad...my mom said we shouldn't trust him. Not about Novalee anyway."

"What? Why would she say that?"

"I don't know, Jess. She didn't say."

"I mean, my dad's harsh, sure, but he wouldn't do anything to deliberately hurt anyone."

She nodded, taking a sip of her coffee and leaning across the island toward him. "I know. I believe that. I'm just relaying the message."

"Why didn't you ask her what she meant?"

"She was being cautious, so I couldn't push. I don't think she wanted Dad to hear her saying anything bad about Big Jim."

He nodded, that made sense, but still, something

didn't sit right with him. He reached out, taking her hand. It was shaking. "What's wrong?"

"I need to say something, Jess. I need to say it, and I don't want you to hate me."

"Hate you?" He gulped. "Why would I hate you?" This was it. She was calling it quits already. One night of happiness for his world to implode back into its usual dullness.

"I, um, well...we both know how much I love Nancy Drew, but I've never considered myself a detective by any means." She tried to smile, but he couldn't smile back. He was completely frozen by fear.

"Spit it out, Q, you're scaring me."

She took a breath, puffing it out with her mouth in the shape of an 'O.' "It's just...I've been thinking. Ever since your mom told us that story about Nova. And the baby." She paused, staring into her coffee. "And the father."

"Yeah?"

She twisted her lips, pushing them out. "She said Novalee was having the baby by a married man."

"Are you worried about that? Because of us?" Relief washed over him as he realized what she was saying. "You don't have to worry about Nova. I know the baby confuses things, but I don't have feelings for her in that way. Just because she doesn't have respect for relationships doesn't mean I don't. I promise you, you don't have anything to worry about. I love *you*," he insisted.

"No," she said, shaking her head. "No, that's not what I mean. I'm wondering who the father was."

"What?"

She winced. "I'm wondering if it was Big Jim." His heart pounded in his chest, cold chills running over him. He opened his mouth, closed it, and opened again.

"Think about it: he knows so much about the pregnancy. And your parents were adamantly against you seeing her. Maybe they're worried she'll tell you something they don't want you to know."

He shook his head. "No. No way. *No way.* It's not possible. You've got it all wrong. He wouldn't. "

"I thought the same about my dad, too," she said, squinting her eyes in pain.

"It's different. Mine..."

"What? What makes your parents immune to the very thing that splits up over half the marriages in America?"

He bit down on his tongue. "My parents are happy."

She shrugged. "Okay, well, it was just a thought."

He touched her hand. "Thank you for looking out for me. I just can't see that it would be possible."

She kissed his nose, pushing his hair back from his face. "I've always got your back, stud." She winked. He tried to smile at her, yet the sick feeling in his gut wasn't fading. There was no way she could be right...could she?

THIRTY-EIGHT

JESSE

After Quinn had left for work, Jesse headed to Nova's house, his stomach bubbling with worry. He walked up to her door and knocked carefully. What Quinn had suggested was ridiculous. There was no way his father would have had an affair—and certainly not with Novalee.

Still, he couldn't wipe the look on Novalee's face when he told her who his father was out of his mind. Or the look on his father's face when he'd said Novalee's name. He shuddered. *No.* It wasn't possible. It was the most ridiculous thing he'd ever heard, and he was going to put it to rest once and for all.

She answered the door, her long dark hair in a low ponytail, a silk robe wrapped around her small frame. "Jesse?"

"We need to talk."

She stepped back, allowing him into the house with a worried look on her face. "What's going on?"

"I need to ask you something." He wagged a finger at her but pulled it back as she placed a hand on her hip, staring at him testily. "And you need to tell me the truth."

"Okay," she agreed. He tried to study her expression, but he didn't know her well enough to read it—she wasn't Quinn.

"It's none of my business, Nova. I realize that, but I'm asking anyway. I need the truth."

"Just get on with it, Jesse." She rolled her eyes.

"Who was the father of your first baby?"

She lowered her brows. "What have you been told?"

"Why won't you answer?" he demanded.

"Because you're right," she snapped. "It *is* none of your business."

"Was it my dad?" he asked, fear overtaking his anger.

Her eyes grew wide. *"What?"* A laugh escaped her throat. "Oh, god, Jesse. No. No, no, no." She waved her hands in front of her face like a windshield.

"He wasn't?"

"No," she said with a scrunched nose as if she'd smelled something bad. "Why on earth would you think that?"

"Because...because you both seem to hate each other."

"That's because *we do.* But not because we had some crazy affair. Your dad always hated me. We ran around in two completely different crowds, and it seemed as though I personally offended him by merely existing." She smirked. "I would *never ever* have slept with your father. And I'm sure he'd say the same."

For the first time all day, he felt true relief wash over him, taking a deep breath. "Oh, thank god."

"Now, that would've been twisted, right?" she said with a snort, patting her knee.

"Yeah, you've got that right. But, if not my dad, then who?"

She waved her hand. "Ah, just a guy I went to high school with."

"Was it—was he married?"

She looked down. "Yes, at the time that I'd gotten pregnant, he was married. I was a stupid young girl that believed him when he said his marriage was over. That he loved me more."

"So, that was why you decided not to have the baby?"

She shook her head. "No. I loved that baby. It was a piece of Rick. Even if I never got to keep him, I wanted her."

"Rick?" he asked, his throat suddenly dry.

"The father. You probably don't know him."

"Rick who?" His heart was speeding up again, and he hoped to god she was right. Dale was a small town, but there was only one Rick he could think of.

"Rick James," she said, confirming his fears. "He died a few years ago. Like I said, you probably don't know him."

"I do know him," he told her, his jaw tight. Rick James was Gunner's father. Gunner was the man Reagan had left him for. Did Gunner know about the affair? Did his mother? "I remember when Rick died. His son, the one that's still living, he just married my ex-fiancée."

She shook her head, making a 'tsk-tsk' noise. "Gotta love small towns."

"Did Rick's family know? About you and the baby?"

"I don't know. If they do, it'd be news to me. He loved his wife, Jesse. He made that clear. Honestly, I hadn't heard from him in years when the news of his death made its way to me."

"So, then...you...were you suicidal?" He winced as he said the word. "Were you suicidal when he broke it off? Is that why you...you know. Not judging," he said quickly, "honestly. I'm just trying to understand."

She was slow to answer, looking at her hands with a serious expression on her face. "Jesse, I don't remember that night. I don't know what I did or didn't do. But, I didn't want to die, and I certainly didn't want my baby to die. I had been sober throughout my whole pregnancy, which was incredible for me. Even losing Rick, as painful as it was, didn't feel like enough to do what they say I did. I'll never understand it."

"But then why would you try to sue the hospital?

Her forehead wrinkled in surprise. "They told you about that?"

He nodded.

She stood up, running a hand over her robe, obviously agitated. "They, they made me sign a non-disclosure. Those records were supposed to be sealed. Your dad promised—"

"*My dad?*"

"Yes, of course. Who else could've told you?"

"Well, my dad told me, but he said...he didn't tell me he was involved. He made it sound like my grandfather did it all."

She sat back down, fingertips on her lips. "Oh, well, maybe I'm just confused. It's been so long."

"Nova, you don't have to lie to me. I'll protect you from whatever you're worried about. My dad won't be suing you for telling me the truth, I can promise you that."

"It doesn't matter anymore, Jesse. It was so long ago."

"It matters to me."

She pressed her lips together, her eyes suddenly swimming with tears. "I tried to sue because I didn't believe their story."

"What story? Whose?"

"Any of what they told me. My doctors. I didn't believe I was capable of the monstrous things they were accusing me of. One minute I was at a bar with Diane Norwood and her husband. They'd invited me to their table, but I only remember ordering a coke. The rest of the night is a blur until I woke up the next day. I knew it the second I opened my eyes—that she was gone. My stomach hurt so badly, but somehow I could only focus on how empty I felt. I tried to sit up, but it hurt. Oh, god, it felt like my insides were being ripped out. Doctor Norwood told me I'd gotten drunk and agitated and tried to kill myself and my baby." She wiped a tear from her eye, sniffling. "But I didn't—couldn't—believe it."

"So, what are you saying? I don't understand."

"I thought they...I don't know. I don't know what I thought. But it hurt too much to believe it. To believe them." Her body shook, tears rolling down her ashen cheeks, her hands moving to cover her eyes.

"Nova, I'm so sorry. I didn't realize—"

"No, because it's not the story they spin. I tried to get more info, proof of what they were telling me, but your father shut me down. He offered me money to shut up," she said with a scoff. "Twenty five hundred dollars. Like that was what my daughter's life was worth. When I didn't take it, the hospital started threatening me with slander. The doctors, the town, they know my story. We aren't far enough away from Dale for me to escape that. I was no saint—"

"That doesn't give them a right to do what they did. Doctors don't care about social status. It's our job to protect you."

"It doesn't matter, Jesse. Old men and their money...they run this world, haven't you heard?"

Jesse rubbed his jaw. He couldn't believe what she was saying, yet the tears in her eyes screamed honesty. "Nova, that's not true."

"It is. You will be one of those men one day. It's in your blood." She smiled at him sadly.

"No," he spat out. "No way. I'll never be that way. I care about my patients. I would never hurt one of them to protect my reputation. I'm not my father."

She patted his hand as if he were a child. "It's okay, Jesse, honestly. I don't like to dwell on it, and you shouldn't either. I'm older and stronger now. We can't change the past. I just want this baby to be healthy for you."

"It will be," he said, placing a hand on the small bump that now protruded from her lower abdomen.

"You can't promise that. I'm so scared I'll do something stupid again. I'm terrified they'll come after me if I do. This is Big Jim's grandchild I'm carrying. If something happens—"

"Nothing is going to happen. My dad isn't some mafia boss. He's an average guy. He mows the grass on Sundays, he's mayor of a town of less than eight hundred. He never went to college. Our money comes from his father. He doesn't have the resources or power to do anything to you. He may have a temper, and his reputation is important to him, but he's...he's not a monster, Nova."

She didn't look as though he'd put her at ease. "I hope you're right."

He stood up, pulling her up with him and wrapping her in a hug. "I will keep you safe, you and our baby. I don't want you worrying about that."

She nodded, her head bobbing against his shoulder. "Would you," she paused, "would you consider staying here? With me?"

"Staying?" He took a step back.

"I mean, at least for now. While I'm supposed to be on bed rest. It's just hard, living alone at the moment. It's hard to stay in bed when I need things. I won't ask you to do much, though, just be here more than anything."

He looked down, not sure what to say. It didn't feel

right. Not after everything with Quinn had started going so well.

"It was a stupid idea," she said before he could respond. "Forget I said anything. It's these pregnancy hormones, I swear."

"No," he said quickly. "No. It's not stupid. I'm sorry, I just...I'll be here for you however I can. I'd be happy to stay with you until you feel okay on your own. But, I need to talk to Quinn about it first."

"Quinn? Why?" She stared at him.

"Because, I, well, I think we're together now."

"*Together* together? I thought you said you were just friends?"

"I did. We were. But...that's changing."

She scoffed. "How convenient."

"Excuse me?"

"Nothing. Nevermind."

"No, don't be upset. She knows how important this baby is to me. She will understand."

Nova rolled her eyes, looking away. "Just this baby, then. Not me."

"What?" He'd heard what she said, but he wasn't sure what she could mean.

"How important this baby is to you. Not the woman carrying it. I'm just the vessel, right?"

"Nova, what are you—"

"I'm not some whiny girl, Jesse. I am a strong, independent woman. I don't pine for boys half my age. I don't sit up at night dreaming about the possibility of us. You were *not* in my plan. But, you happened, and now I have all these feelings—"

"Feelings for me?" He was utterly lost.

She nodded. "It's not like I want them," she said quickly. "God, I hate feeling this way. I am not the type to be vulnerable. But, I can't make them go away and then, everything with the baby happened and...I don't know. I can't help but wondering what our little family could be."

"*Family*? I thought you didn't want to be a part of this baby's life." He blinked slowly, feeling bewildered. What in the world was going on?

"I don't. I mean, I don't know what I want. I told you our story wouldn't have a happy ending, and I meant it. At the time. But, now I'm just confused. I don't know what I want. But, I do know the further along I get," she paused, grabbing his hand and placing it on her belly. "The more our baby grows inside of me, the more I think about it. About us." She studied him, her eyes darting back and forth between his.

He pulled his hand back slowly. "Nova, I—"

"I'm sorry," she said, scratching her forehead. "I know this can't be what you want to hear. But, in fairness, you didn't tell me about Quinn. That's your own fault. Maybe being up front about your feelings for her could've saved us both a lot of trouble."

He rubbed his scalp, sighing. "You're right, and I'm sorry for that. I do care about you, Novalee. You and the baby. Just—"

"Just not like you care about Quinn." She nodded, her lips pressed into a tight line.

He exhaled through his nose, looking up. It was a confirmation and she seemed to realize it. She held her arm out, one hand on the growing bump. "I'll see you out now, Jesse. I'd rather be alone."

"I don't want to leave. Not while you're upset."

She ignored him, walking toward the door. "Trust me, I'll be fine. There are worse things than getting turned down by you. On a list of all my bad days, this doesn't even hit top fifty."

He followed her, stopping at the door and placing a hand on her shoulder. He kissed her forehead carefully. "I'll be back to check on you. Take care of yourself, okay?"

She smiled, pressing her lips to his for only a second. He didn't pull away. "You too, Jesse."

THIRTY-NINE

QUINN

She was running out of time. Ever since Jesse had told her about Nova's records being sealed and admitted the true reason for wanting to see them, she'd been trying to come up with a plan to find them. Jesse wouldn't survive losing this child—and if finding her records could help him prevent that in some way, she had to find them.

The chief of surgery was the only one who might have a copy of the records besides the legal department. If the legal team were the only ones with a copy, she knew there was no way to get her hands on them. Of course, the other option was that they'd been destroyed, and if that was the case there was absolutely no chance of anyone ever seeing them. She severely hoped that wasn't the case. If it was, it would make for a long five months of worrying.

So, there she stood, hurrying around the chief's office,

scouring through his files. The password to his computer was unobtainable, so she had resorted to sifting through the old filing cabinets. Chances were, anything from so long ago was likely kept on paper anyway. If a record was sealed, they wouldn't have transferred it over to digital, would they?

She turned his keys over in her hand. It was a miracle that she'd gotten them. Janise had managed to pull them from his coat pocket without him noticing, something Quinn would've never been able to do. Now, Janise stood watch at the end of the hall, ready to give a signal if he started her way.

Of all the people in the hospital, Janise Tedlock was the last person she expected to help her. The oldest of all the residents, and a rather uptight woman in general, Janise mostly kept to herself, but when she noticed Quinn's distracted state, she'd had no choice but to open up about what was going on. To her surprise, Janise had been all too excited to help her 'take the bastards down'— her words. So much so, Quinn couldn't help but wonder if this might be some sort of trap. She cast the thought away quickly, not having time to prepare or worry. If she were caught, no amount of backstory or excuse could help her avoid being fired or possible jail time. But Jesse was worth it, no doubt about that. He would do it for her if the situation were reversed.

The filing cabinet she was going through now had old papers, records from before their conversion to digital, blueprints of the hospital, and bills. She smiled when she saw William Mathis' signature on a few—Jesse's grandfather. She was on the right track.

She flipped through the old hanging folders, searching through the folders for 'P' and 'N' to no avail. As she was just about to give up, she searched the 'C' folder for confidential and finally the 'S' folder for sealed. Her eyes lit up as she saw Novalee's name in the top right hand corner of a page.

She pulled it out, smiling to herself as her eyes darted over the page. It wasn't a medical record, but rather a non-disclosure agreement, signed by Novalee and William Mathis, as well as two members of the legal team. She read through it carefully, stopping on the date of which Nova's baby had died. *What?* She read over it again. *No.*

She turned around, shutting the cabinet and hurrying from the office. Janise was waiting for her at the end of the hall. "Did you find what you were looking for?"

"I don't know," Quinn said, not offering to show her the paper. She still wasn't sure what to make of her discovery. "Maybe. I hope so."

Janise nodded. "You get 'em girl," she said.

"I need to leave," Quinn told her. "But my shift doesn't end for another three hours."

Janise frowned. "I'll talk to the girls and get your patients covered. You know, we wouldn't want you to infect anyone with your *sudden illness.*"

Quinn tilted her head to the side. "Not that I'm not grateful, because I couldn't have done this without you, but why are you helping me? We've never really been friends."

"You know, they say more women have lost a baby than haven't." She touched her stomach, staring at Quinn with haunted eyes. Quinn nodded, wanting to apologize but feeling unable to form the words. "If I can save even one woman from that pain, all of this is worth it."

QUINN WALKED into Jesse's house, surprised that he wasn't still at hers. "Jess?" she called. "Jess, where are you? I thought you'd be at my house."

Suddenly, she could hear him shuffling around in the kitchen. "Jess, I found something you need to see. It's about Novalee. I...I don't know what to think. It could be nothing, but—"

She stopped dead at seeing who was waiting for her in the kitchen. "You—" she said, her lips quivering. *Danger.* She was in danger. She knew that as she stood frozen, staring at an expression she'd never seen on a face she knew so well.

"Well, well, well, what do we have here?"

FORTY

JESSE

Jesse had arrived back at Quinn's house in the early afternoon. When he realized she wasn't going to make it home for dinner, he laid on the couch—waiting for her while watching a bit of television.

When he woke up the next morning, though, and she still wasn't home, he began to worry. He sent her a quick text before hopping in the shower, but when he got out and she still hadn't texted him back, he knew something was wrong. First, he checked the hospital.

"No, I'm sorry, Jesse, Quinn isn't here. She left last night around seven," one of the nurses told him over the phone. "Do you want to leave a message in case she comes in? I can try to get it to her."

"No, that's all right. I'll keep trying her cell," he said, ending the call. He called her mom next. It was drastic, he knew, but his worry was continuing to amplify.

"Hello?" Shelly's voice came over the line.

"Mrs. Reynolds, it's Jesse."

"Jesse, what is it?" Concern filled her voice. "Is everything all right?"

"I, um, did Quinn come there last night?"

"No," she said, "why? Has something happened?"

"I don't know." He could hear her shuffling around. "She didn't come home last night, and she isn't answering my texts."

"Have you two had a fight?"

"No," he insisted. "Not that I know of."

"Have you checked the hospital? Maybe she picked up an extra shift."

"Yeah, I checked there first, she's already gone."

"Oh, god. *Marcus*," she called out. Her voice was quickly muffled, and Jesse was sure she'd covered the speaker. He could hardly hear her hushed tones. "Jesse, where are you now?" she asked, her voice coming back into focus.

"I'm at her house."

"Have you checked your house yet?"

"No, but I don't know why she'd go there. She knew I'd be here."

"Okay, Jesse, listen to me carefully, you stay put, okay? Don't leave her house, and I want you to call me right away if you hear from her. Do you understand?"

"Yes, I do, but why? Do you have an idea of what's going on?"

"I hope not," she said, her tone ominous. "We'll talk

soon." With that, the line went dead and he was left alone to fear the worst.

AFTER AN HOUR HAD PASSED without a word, Jesse was done waiting. He felt cruel doing it, but if Quinn was in danger, it was well worth it. He'd do anything to save her. Anything. And so, he turned to the only person in the world he thought might be able to help.

"Hello?" her groggy voice filled the line.

"Nova, it's me."

"Jesse? What is it? What's wrong?"

"I know you're the last person I should ask about this, but I can't help feeling this all comes back to you somehow. You're the connection I can't seem to make fit."

"What are you talking about?" She seemed annoyed.

"Quinn's missing."

"Missing? What do you mean 'missing'?"

"She didn't come home after work last night."

"Oh no. Did you call the police?"

"No," he said, the idea only occurring to him then. "Should I?"

"I don't know, but 'missing' sounds bad. Do you think she could be in danger? Or did you just have a fight?"

"We weren't fighting," he said defensively, not allowing himself to fully consider the other option.

"Have you checked with her friends? Family?"

"I'm her friend. It's just me and her. She has a few

girls from work she talks to but no one close enough to leave work with. She wouldn't have gone anywhere else. She knew I would be here waiting for her after she got off anyway, so if her plans had changed, she would've told me. And her parents haven't heard from her either."

"Okay. It sounds like you need to call the police, Jesse. Hopefully she's safe, but you can't find her on your own."

A phone call began beeping in over the call before he could respond. "Hang on just a second, okay? I'm getting another call." He selected the green answer button on his screen, praying it would be her. "Hello?"

"Jesse?" He recognized the voice, though he couldn't place it.

"Yeah, who is this?"

"It's Tedlock. From the hospital."

Calling him in to work, no doubt. "Oh, hey," he said. There was no way in hell he was going in until Quinn was found.

"Um, Quinn didn't show up for her shift today. Brittany said you were looking for her."

"Yeah, I can't get ahold of her, and she never came home last night after her shift."

"Right," she said, lowering her voice. "Well, on the record, she went home sick yesterday."

"Sick?"

"On the record, Mathis. Pay attention."

"Right. So, what's the truth? Off the record."

"I don't know if I should be telling you this. But, I'm worried about her. I know you two are close."

"She's my best friend, Janise. Please tell me whatever it is you know." His heart was pounding in his chest.

"Quinn told me about the complications with your, for lack of a better word, *baby mama's* pregnancy. She was determined to find some sealed records, seemed to think that was important to you, so we distracted Chief Norwood, just long enough for her to search his office."

"You did *what*? What happened?"

"Well, I didn't think it was anything. She left with a paper, she didn't say what it was and I didn't ask. She wanted to go home right after, so I covered for her."

"Okay, what time was that?"

"Um, around seven."

"No one's seen or heard from her in nearly eighteen hours then."

"Jesse, that's not all."

"Okay, go on."

"After she left, I turned to go down the hallway but the chief caught me. He wanted to know what I was doing still by his office."

"And what did you tell him?" He paced the living room, taking in her every word.

"I made up some lame excuse about coming to see how things went with the patient I'd asked him to talk to. I don't know if believed me. He seemed to, but then when Quinn didn't show up, I started to worry. And then the chief didn't show up either. What if he found out we'd been snooping? What if whatever Quinn found was something he didn't want her to? Am I being crazy? Maybe I've just watched one too many episodes of *CSI*."

He grabbed his keys from the coffee table. "No. You were right to tell me. Thank you for doing this, Janise, and for helping her. I'll check into the chief."

"I just don't want her to get hurt."

"I'm going to find her," he promised. When he switched back over, Nova was gone.

FORTY-ONE

JESSE

Jesse pounded on the Norwood's door. After a few moments, the chief's wife, Diane, appeared.

"What in the world—" She stopped, staring at him. Her graying dark hair was clipped back away from her face, and she wore a faded purple jumpsuit. "Jesse?" She recognized him instantly. Growing up, every weekend had been spent with the Norwoods and Reynolds at his house. They were his parents' best friends, but the visits had grown less frequent as the years passed.

"Is the chief here?" Even though he'd known him outside of work first, he still found it impossible to call Greg Norwood anything but 'chief' now.

"No, Jesse, I'm afraid he's not. He should be at the hospital. What's going on?" She lowered her brow.

"Where is she?" he demanded, through with the small talk.

"Where is who?"

"Quinn. Is she here? What has he done with her?"

"What on earth are you talking about?" Her jaw dropped open as she shook her head.

"Quinn is missing, Diane, and I think, no I *know,* you guys know where she is."

She touched her mouth with her fingertips. "Quinn Reynolds is missing?"

"Yes." His fists were clenched at his sides, his whole body tense. Minutes and hours were just ticking by with him helpless to save her.

"Jesse, come inside," she whispered hurriedly, placing a hand on his back. He didn't have time to think how bad of an idea that could be as he allowed her to usher him into the house. When she shut the door, she eyed him carefully, crossing her arms. "Now, why do you think Greg and I have anything to do with Quinn going missing? And when did you realize she was gone?"

"Quinn and I have been searching for answers regarding a patient who had a miscarriage years ago. A patient your husband, Doctor Reynolds, and my grandfather operated on. They tried to run her out of town afterward, treated her like dirt. We want to know why. I don't know if there was malpractice involved or if they just hated her that much, but we were determined to find out. And yesterday, Quinn found something. Something they didn't want her to find, apparently. And, now she's missing."

Did he detect a hint of fear in her eyes? "Jesse, when did you discover Quinn was missing?"

He hesitated.

"Was it around ten or eleven this morning?"

He nodded. "You do know what's happened to her then, don't you?" She rushed to the table in the hall, opening up a drawer and sifting through a stack of papers. "What are you looking for? What's going on?" he asked, approaching her.

She shook her head, obviously agitated. "There's so much you don't know, Jesse, and god knows it's not my place to tell you. But, what's most important right now is that we find Quinn before they do something stupid."

He stepped forward. "Who is 'they'? What are you talking about? Do you know where she is?"

"I have an idea, yes." She still wasn't looking his direction, thumbing through stacks upon stacks of papers lining the wooden drawer.

"Where?" he demanded.

She snatched a yellow paper from the drawer, holding it up in the air and turning to face him. "Our safe house."

FORTY-TWO

QUINN

Darkness. Cold. She was surrounded by both. Quinn forced her heavy eyelids open. *Where was she?*

There were voices in the distance, beyond the darkness, but she was having trouble making them out. She sat up, blinking as her eyes tried to adjust to the pitch-black room. There were no traces of light anywhere. The ground underneath her was ice cold concrete.

She ran her hands over the dirty floor, moving inch by inch toward the voices. She stopped when she hit something solid, running her hands along the wooden step until they fell through the crack. She lifted her knee up, placing it onto the wood.

Slowly, one careful step at a time, she made her way up the staircase, her hands guiding the way. After nineteen steps, she had reached the top, broken linoleum tiles under her fingers leading up to a door with a bit of light escaping at its bottom. She leaned her ear up to it, a steady flow of heat escaping from the gap under the door. She placed her fingertips in front of the gap, warming them slightly. ·

"What choice do we have? This was never part of the plan." His booming voice made her jump. The voice belonged to the chief of surgery, Greg Norwood.

"Going to jail certainly wasn't part of the plan, either," Big Jim retorted indignantly. She winced as she heard his voice again, moving her hands to the lump on her forehead. She had forgotten. When she'd entered the house, Big Jim had been waiting, for Jesse presumably, but once he'd seen what she had and figured out what she only had suspicions of at the time, he'd attacked, hitting her over the head with a coffee mug. She'd woken up only once since then but sleep found her quickly that time. She wasn't sure how much time had passed, or exactly how much longer she might be there.

"I'll take the fall for everything. I'll say it was all me. They don't know about the others. Please. *Please,* Jim, just let me take her home." This voice surprised her. It was her father's. *What on earth was he doing there?*

"No. I'm sorry, Marcus, Shelly—it's too much of a liability."

Shelly. Was her mother there, too? Answering her question, she heard her snappy response. "*It?* She, Jim. She. Our daughter is not an 'it.'"

"We can explain to her what we've done and why. We can tell her what could happen if anyone finds out."

"No. We agreed years ago that the six of us, seven

including Dad, were all that could ever know. Six is too many, if you ask me, but we had no choice," Big Jim roared.

"We have no choice now, either. What are you proposing? And what about *your* son? It's his promiscuity that's gotten us into this mess in the first place," Shelly argued. "Why should my daughter have to pay for his mistakes?"

"She's paying for sticking her nose where it doesn't belong."

"To protect your boy," Marcus exclaimed, his voice broken.

"They're in love, Jim. Has Jesse told you that? How will you explain to him what you've done to the woman he loves?" Shelly begged. "They're just children, they have no idea what they're getting themselves into."

To that, Big Jim seemed to have no response. "Look, I don't like this any more than you all do. But, it is what it is. Quinn is like a daughter to me as well. I'm trying to protect all of us—not just myself."

"I don't care about being saved," Shelly bellowed, sobs in her voice. "I care about Quinn's life."

Life? Quinn shifted in her place, shaking her leg to wake it from sleep. Was she truly in that much danger? Big Jim was right—she'd always considered him a second father, could he really want her dead?

"We didn't do this to hurt anybody," Greg said, so soft Quinn almost hadn't heard it.

"Oh, who are we kidding? We were hurting people, and we all knew it. It's just that none of you care until it's you who stands to be hurt. This was never a victimless crime. We all knew that going in," Big Jim said, his voice dripping with arrogance.

"Enough," Shelly said. "There's no sense in arguing over what can't be changed. Quinn can still be saved. We will take the fall, we've said. We'll tell them it was only us. Just let her out."

"And when she hears the truth? What then? Do you really think she'll be so quick to forgive you?"

"At least she'll be alive to make that decision," she screeched.

"Be quiet," Greg said suddenly. "Someone's coming." The room grew silent and Quinn was very aware of the sound of her breathing. Tiredness was beginning to overtake her once again, and she considered crawling back down the stairs. The last thing she needed was to fall asleep and tumble down. "It's Diane," Greg said after a few minutes. "And someone's following her."

After a bit, she heard her voice. "What the hell do you people think you're doing?" Diane demanded.

"Diane, honey, what are you doing? How'd you know where we'd be?" Greg asked.

"What's he doing here?" Big Jim asked. *He who?*

"Dad," Jesse said. "Diane told me everything."

Relief washed over her at hearing Jesse's voice. He was sad, maybe mad, she couldn't be sure, but either way she didn't have time to dwell on it. Now was her chance.

With all of her might, she pounded on the door in front of her. "Jesse! Jesse, please!" she screamed, her voice dry and cracking. She heard heavy footsteps barreling toward her at lightning speed.

"Quinn?" he called, his voice closer to her. "Where is she?"

"Jesse, wait," Big Jim yelled, and suddenly more footsteps were headed her way.

"Jesse, I'm here!" she called again, her mouth pressed into the door. She slid back, inching her way onto the next step down as his footsteps grew closer. His voice was just beyond the wood. "Is she in here?" He pounded on the door. "Quinn?"

"Yes, I'm here. It's me," she cried.

"Don't open that door, son. You don't understand."

The knob twisted and light filled the room, burning her eyes. She put a hand up. "I understand perfectly. You aren't going to lay a finger on her," Jesse said, taking a step forward. He bent down, touching her face. "Are you okay?" He wrapped her in a hug, tears filling her eyes instantly. "I've been so worried about you."

"Jesse, your dad—"

"I know," he said, putting his arm around her. "Can you stand? We have to get you out of here."

She nodded, leaning her weight onto him and allowing him to pull her up. Her legs were stiff but she could stand on them.

"What did you do, Diane? Cherie will have a fit when she finds out you've told Jesse," Big Jim exclaimed, his eyes darting back and forth between Quinn and Jesse as they exited the basement.

"I saved Quinn's life," she said proudly. "And probably doomed us all. Now you have no choice—if you want to do anything to that child, you'll have to do the same to your own. He knows everything, every dirty detail. I made sure of it."

Shelly made a whimper, pulling her daughter into her arms and stroking her hair. Fat tears poured down her cheeks. Her parents surrounded her, their sobs loud in her ears.

"Greg, your wife has lost her mind," Big Jim said angrily.

"No, Jim," Greg argued. "She did the right thing." He stepped in front of her protectively. "This was never in the plan. We did what we did out of love, selfish as that may have been. And I think it's time we face the consequences. Unless, of course, you plan to kill your own son as well as Quinn. And, if that's the case, you may as well kill us all. Or we'll take you down trying. This secret is too much for us now. It's the kids' choice what they want to do with it. I'm done letting you push me around."

"Well, I—er—this is crap—you—" Big Jim muttered and grumbled under his breath, defeated.

"What's it going to be, Dad? Are you letting us go, or is keeping your secret important enough to kill for?"

"What secret?" Quinn asked, still waiting for her theory to be confirmed.

Jesse opened his mouth. "Twenty-eight years ago, our families—"

"No," Shelly spoke up, letting go of Quinn. "No, Jesse."

"She has a right to know."

"Yes, she does," she agreed. "But, we'd like to be the ones to tell her."

Jesse shrugged. "As long as someone does."

Big Jim closed his giant red fists. "Fine," he huffed. "But, if we tell her, you're both sworn to secrecy. You'd be accomplices. If one of us goes down, we all do." He was grasping at straws, and everyone seemed to know it, though no one agreed to his terms. Instead, Shelly sat down in a nearby chair and asked Quinn to do the same. Quinn would've preferred to stand, but her concussion was making it harder than ever to stay awake.

"Could we have some privacy please?" Marcus asked, perched beside Shelly on the arm of a small couch.

No one bothered to move. Jesse crossed his arms, feet planted in the green carpet. "I'm staying to make sure you tell her everything."

Shelly nodded. "I suppose that's fair." She turned back to Quinn. "Quinnie," she said, with tears welling in her eyes once again. "What you probably suspect based on the non-disclosure agreement you found is true."

Quinn bit her lips, unable to say the words.

Her mother closed her eyes, furrowing her brow as she said the words Quinn hoped she'd been wrong about. "Novalee Phillips is your birth mother."

FORTY-THREE

QUINN

"What?" Quinn asked, though her mother was right, the suspicion had been there from the time she'd seen the baby's death date matched her own birthdate. Her parents had always blamed the lack of pregnancy pictures on a fire that happened shortly after Quinn was born. She'd never thought to question it. "But, Nova...she...why?" she asked. It was the only question she could muster.

"It was Big Jim's idea initially, but he was doing it to help us, so I guess it's still our fault. Your father and I, we wanted a baby, wanted *you* so badly. But, we found out kids weren't in the picture for us. We'd never be able to have a child of our own. It was the hardest thing, Quinn. It destroyed us—it would've destroyed our marriage. And Novalee, she was pregnant *by accident.* I hated her so much for accidentally getting what I'd painstakingly tried and failed at. So, we did what people do and we started weighing our options. We looked into adoption, but your father was fresh out of medical school with bills sky high and we were barely making it on my teacher's salary. There was no way we could've afforded it."

"You couldn't afford it, so you just stole her baby? You stole me?" Her breathing was growing erratic.

"I know what you must think of us, how awful this all sounds. We...it's not easy for us to tell you any of this. There's no way to word it so we don't sound like criminals," Shelly said sadly.

"Novalee wasn't fit to be a mother, Quinn. Your life would've been ruined if we'd let her keep you," Marcus added.

"You don't get to decide that," Quinn said through gritted teeth. "You don't have any say in what a fit parent is. Not anymore." She let out a breath. "What did you do?" she demanded, fear filling her. It was as if she were staring into the faces of strangers, the oddest feeling.

"We...drugged Novalee," Shelly said, her face showing she'd never had to say those words aloud. "We invited her out for drinks. I thought I would feel better if she ordered alcohol, like it would be further proof that she didn't deserve you, but she didn't. We'd heard she and Rick James had broken up, so we knew we had to act, even though you weren't quite ready to be born." She paused, looking up at Marcus, her expression weary.

He seemed to understand, taking over the storytelling. "After Greg and Diane slipped her the drugs, we brought her to the hospital and Greg and I performed an emergency c-section. William Mathis came in mid-way through. He saved your life, and eventually Big Jim was able to convince him to keep our secret. If William hadn't been there that day, I don't think you would've made it. You were so tiny. We...we were so stupid." He placed his face in his palms.

"So, then what?" Quinn asked, looking to her mother. She needed to hear the rest, unable to process without all of the details.

"After things settled down, we believed we were in the clear. But, Nova wouldn't leave well enough alone. That's why we had her sign the non-disclosure. She threatened to sue, to get attention brought to the hospital that could've jeopardized everything. We told everyone that we had a home birth, and you were so tiny we were able to say that I wasn't showing much. But, there were still plenty of holes in our story. We couldn't afford to have anyone looking at us too closely."

"So, you just destroyed her?" Jesse demanded, rage in his eyes. "She was a kid. A terrified, heartbroken, incredibly alone kid with nowhere to go and nothing, no one, to turn to. She'd lost her boyfriend, her child, and her home all at once, and you people...you didn't care as long as you got what you wanted. *She's a person.* I don't understand how anyone could be so heartless."

"We were horrible," Diane spoke up. "There's no excuse for what we did. We wanted to save Shelly and Marcus the heartache of being childless, consequences be damned. The secret has eaten me up everyday, your mother, too, Jesse. Hell, all of us. Except you," she said, eyeing Jim. "And I wish it ended there." She looked down, shoulders slumped.

"What do you mean?" Quinn asked, since she seemed to be the only one in the room who didn't know.

"After we got you, William got greedy. Big Jim got greedy," Diane said.

"Now, don't you go pointing fingers—" Big Jim started, wagging a sausage-like finger in the air.

"We *all* got greedy," Greg corrected. "Big Jim and William may have come up with the idea, but we were all on board. After all, we'd done it once without getting caught, why couldn't we do it again?"

"More babies? You stole more babies?" Quinn choked out, feeling bile rise in her throat. She placed a hand over her belly.

"Eight total, including you," Shelly told her, reaching for her hand. Quinn jerked away. "We kept them spread out, only went after mothers we deemed unfit."

"What did you do with them? With the babies?"

"We..." Shelly paused.

"Sold them to the highest bidder," Diane finished for her. "Let's call it what it is."

Quinn stood up, looking away from her parents. "This is sick. Awful. Disgusting. Those words aren't good enough to describe what you've done. You...you people are monsters. You had no right to do it, why, you're no better than any mothers you might've decided were...what did you call them? Unfit? Who gave you the right to decide that? What could they possibly have done to deserve this? What sin could they have possibly committed that was worse than what you've done?" Quinn curled her lip in disgust, she could feel her pulse in her fingertips, hear it in her ears.

"Nothing, Quinn," her father answered, "absolutely nothing that justified what we did. And you have every right to turn us in."

"We won't stop you," Diane agreed.

Big Jim huffed from the other side of the room, clearly not in agreement but outnumbered nonetheless.

"What excuse do you have, Dad?" Jesse asked. "Was it all about the money?"

Big Jim puffed out his chest, looking at his son. "You couldn't possibly understand." He took a step forward, lowering his voice. "I was never going to be a surgeon, son. Not like you or my father. And he made sure to let me know that, and to remind me of my failure constantly. My father hated me for not having the ambition he had, the ambition I see in you. But, doing this, I was giving good people a proper chance to raise a family. Ones that couldn't have otherwise. Adoption waiting lists are years long, and sometimes the calls never come. I was helping people. And, yeah, I was making money. We all were. You weren't complaining about that money when it was paying for your car or your football or your medical school."

"You're disgusting," Jesse spat. "Don't you dare make me feel guilty for what you've done."

Quinn approached him, sliding her hand into his. "Can we just go, Jesse?"

"Yeah, we can." He nodded, turning to face the door.

Diane and Greg stepped out of the way to allow them passage.

"Now, wait just one damn minute," Big Jim called. "What are you going to do?"

"I don't know," Jesse said, not bothering to stop. "I guess you'll just have to wait and see."

"Son, please—"

Jesse spun around quickly. "You're not my father," he screamed, his face growing red. "Don't *ever* call me that again. I want nothing to do with you. Even if I don't go to the police, you will never hear from me again."

"Jesse." Big Jim's voice was low, he took a step back, obviously caught off guard. "You can't just do that. I'm your father, son. I love you."

"You aren't my father," Jesse repeated. "I've decided you're unfit."

FORTY-FOUR

JESSE

Jesse allowed Quinn to cry the whole way home, the weight of their discovery heavy between them. What could he say? What should he say? He couldn't help but feel guilty for his father's sins against Quinn, though he knew he wasn't at fault. Still, the guilt filled him...guilt for loving the man who had taken so much from the woman he loved, guilt for wearing his eyes so proudly once, for boasting the same smile.

All those years, when his parents had seen Quinn—had the pain of harboring such a dark secret caused them any regret? Jesse doubted it. Big Jim, especially, wasn't one for regrets or pain. He stood by his choices, always had, even when they were terribly wrong.

Jesse was worried about Quinn. Everything in her life had been exposed as a lie...how could he relate to that? How could he expect her to still love him when the blood that coursed through his veins was put there by the man who'd ripped her life away before she'd taken her first breath?

They pulled into Dale, but Jesse didn't bother to drive home, instead pulling over in the town square. He wasn't sure which of their homes she would choose to go to. What if she never wanted to see him again? Could he survive that? He slammed his hand into the steering wheel, pressing his forehead into the shiny leather.

Quinn leaned her head over, falling onto his shoulder. He sighed, wrapping an arm around her and kissing the top of her head. "I'm so sorry, Quinn," he whispered, his voice catching in his throat. Those words weren't enough, but then again, what words ever could be?

She didn't respond at first, her tears soaking through to his skin. He ran a hand over her hair, prepared to sit there all night if that's what she needed. Instead, she surprised him by leaning away from his shoulder, staring up with red eyes. "We have to go tell her the truth."

"Who?"

"Nova," she said simply.

He stared at her. "Are you sure you want to do that? You haven't had time to process yet. There's no reason to rush."

"How much time will be enough, Jess? A day? A week? A year? How much time will be long enough for me to come to terms with the fact that my entire life has been a lie?" She was angry, and he couldn't blame her. When he didn't answer, she went on, "I'm not doing this because of who Nova is, anyway. Biologically, she's my mother, yes, but that's not why I'm doing it. I haven't had time to process, you're right. I'm not sure any amount of time will be enough, but Nova deserves to know the truth. As a person. As a woman. I can't keep this secret from her. It will burst out of me, Jesse. It's too much." She clutched her chest, mascara streaming down her cheeks. "She's carried the pain of her loss, a loss that never even happened and certainly isn't her fault, for so long. Literally, my whole life. Every day that I have been alive, Nova has been suffering. I'm not the victim here. My life has been good. My parents were good to me. But, Nova has known so much pain and unnecessary guilt. So, no matter how much I'm hurting, no matter what I need right now, we have to do the right thing for her."

He nodded, staring at his hands on the steering wheel. "And if she goes to the police? Our parents will go to jail. Is that what we want?"

She looked down, wringing her hands in her lap. "It doesn't matter what we want." Then after a moment, she said, "But, yeah. She should go to the police. Her and the seven others. They deserve justice. We have to tell her everything and let her decide what she wants to do."

He started up the car. "Quinn, you realize all of this means you have half-siblings, right? A half-sibling, at least. Rick James had kids."

"Rick James was my father?" she asked.

He nodded. "I'm sorry, I thought you heard that."

"I hoped it was wrong, or that I'd misunderstood." She frowned, shaking her head. "Rick wasn't a good guy, Jesse. From what I remember about him, he was a total drunk. I didn't know the kids very well, but it seems like they always had bruises on them, three guesses where those came from. He's not exactly someone I'm rushing to claim."

Jesse was silent.

"I don't want to think about my family being anyone other than my parents. I know they're horrible people, Jesse. What they did, it's pure evil, unspeakable."

He nodded. "But they did it for you. For the idea of you."

She bit her lip. "I don't know how I'll ever forgive them."

"You don't have to, but maybe someday you'll find a way." She was quiet, not agreeing, but then...he wasn't sure he expected her to. "You know, from what I've seen, Gunner is actually a decent guy."

"What?" she asked, her eyes squinting with confusion.

"Gunner. I mean, Rick is his father, too, and he turned out okay, I think. I don't remember the twins that much, either. I remember their death...hearing about it when it happened. Gavin always seemed like an okay guy, too, but I don't know." He cleared his throat. "I just...Gunner's okay. Blood doesn't determine who you are. I hope I'm living proof of that."

"Only you could say the man who stole your fiancée from you is a good guy," she said, a slight smile on her face.

"I mean, it wasn't really his fault. It's just what

happened." He grabbed her hand, kissing it. "Besides, it all worked out for the best."

She was quiet for a moment before saying, "What if I don't want to be anything like my blood *or* the people who raised me?"

Without an answer, Jesse squeezed her hand. His were the same people, and in truth, he wasn't sure he wanted to be anything like them, either.

FORTY-FIVE

JESSE

When Nova answered the door, Quinn took a step back, hiding her shoulder behind his. He slid his hand into hers, trying to offer reassurance.

Nova looked relieved. "You found her?"

"You told her?" Quinn asked, her voice slightly defensive.

"I was worried about you," Jesse said, glancing over his shoulder at her, then turned back to Nova. "We need to talk to you."

"Jesse, honestly, I don't think the moving in thing is such a good idea any more. I'm really not in the mood to discuss—"

"Moving in?" Quinn demanded.

Jesse held up a hand. "That's not what this is about. Can we come in?"

Nova nodded, stepping back and allowing them to enter. "What's going on?" she asked.

"We should sit," Jesse warned her, his arm around Quinn's waist. He could see the fear permeating in her eyes. They made their way into the living room, Nova sitting across from them on the faded gray couch. "Nova, when I found Quinn, she was being held captive." He paused, rubbing a hand over her arm. He'd been practicing how this speech would go—knew all of his lines. "By my dad."

"Captive?" Her eyes went wide, hand flew to her mouth. "By your dad? Big Jim? What are you talking about?" She had half a smile on her mouth as if she half expected him to start laughing.

"There's no easy way to say any of this," he said plainly, his palms starting to sweat.

She put a protective hand over her stomach. "Just tell me."

"You were right, Nova. You were right about it not being your fault when you lost your baby. You were right about not trusting the doctor's story. They—my dad, my mom, Doctor Norwood, Doctor Reynolds, and their wives—they stole your baby." His voice caught in his throat as he said the words, knowing the pain he'd be inflicting.

Tears filled her eyes immediately, and he felt moisture lining his own, too. "What?" It seemed to be the only word she could muster.

"They...they drugged you and performed an unnecessary and dangerous c-section on you. Then they lied to you about what had happened, blamed you for what they'd done, and ran you out of town with empty threats. You were a young, scared girl, but you did nothing wrong."

"*But...why?*" she asked in a high-pitched voice, her hands shaking. Her jaw dropped open in a loud sob. "What could I have possibly done to deserve this? What could...what could my baby have done? My precious little girl? Why would they hate me so much they...I don't understand," She stopped, sobs overtaking her words, her shoulders shaking. "How...could they...do that? She was just a baby. Completely innocent. How could they hate me enough to kill my child?"

"They didn't do it because they hated you, Nova. I'm not defending them, what they did, there's not even a word for that level of evil. But, they did it, they *stole* your baby, not killed her, because their friends couldn't have children. They decided they deserved your baby more than you."

"What?" She gasped, her eyes studying him.

"Your child, your daughter, was given away to another family. She wasn't killed."

"What are you saying? My baby is alive? My little girl...she didn't die that night? I didn't hurt her?" She grasped her chest, her fingers leaving pink marks on her pale skin. Her breaths were coming shorter and quicker, and Jesse was beginning to fear she may be having a panic attack.

He climbed to the floor, on his knees in front of her. "Nova, breathe. I need you to breathe for me."

She stood up, holding her head. "This feels like some horrible dream. Your parents...I don't understand. They just told you all of this? Why? Why would they do that?"

"To save me," Quinn said, speaking up for the first time. "To protect me."

"You?" she asked. "Oh, *that's right*. They had you held hostage. Why?"

"Because I found something they didn't want me to see. Something that made me suspicious." She took a deep breath. "I found your non-disclosure agreement. And the day that you believed your daughter died—the day my dad operated on you—was also the day I was born."

Novalee stared at her, processing. "What?"

Quinn nodded slowly. "I'm your biological child," she said matter-of-factly. "My parents couldn't have children of their own. So, they stole me from you."

For a moment, Jesse thought Nova may pass out. She held her breath, eyelids fluttering, her mouth in a tight line. "You are?" she asked finally, exhaling.

Quinn gave a short, quick nod.

Novalee's chin began to quiver, her eyes swimming with fresh tears. "Oh, sweetheart." She wiped her tears as quickly as they fell, frozen in her seat. "I wanted you."

Quinn pressed her lips together, her own eyes glistening. "I know," she squeaked.

"They wouldn't...they wouldn't even let me see you, after they said you'd died. I never got to hold you or kiss your sweet face. I'd spent so long imagining what your face would look like. You were old enough for a funeral, I researched it. But, I was never allowed to have one. They told me they'd 'disposed' of you. I was...they said I was too fragile to see you." Her eyes were haunted by the memory. "I wanted you," she repeated. "You were my angel."

"I can't tell you how sorry I am," Quinn offered, "for what my parents did. I can't imagine what you've gone through."

Nova touched her mouth. "You're so beautiful," she whispered, "and healthy?"

Quinn smiled sadly. "I'm very healthy."

"And they were...were they good to you? Did they treat you fairly?"

"They were, *are,* good parents. Yes."

Nova let out a sigh. "I don't know if I would've been a good mom. I was alone, but I never wanted that for you. When Rick and I broke up, I had a plan. It was going to be us against the world." She wiped her eyes. "Just you and me. My sweet little girl." She wiped her nose. "But, maybe they saved you from me. Maybe I would've been worse than them. I could never have given you as much as a doctor's family."

"What they did to you wasn't okay, Nova. Neither is what they did to Quinn. It was illegal. No matter what kind of mom you would have been, they had no right making that decision for you. You have rights now."

"Rights? What do you mean?"

"You could go to the police. You could have them arrested. We'll back you up."

She nodded slowly. "You would let me do that?"

"We want you to do whatever you decide is best for you. No one should be allowed to take that decision away from you—not after everything that's already been taken from you," he said, moving back up to the couch beside Quinn.

"But, if I press charges, you both lose your parents." She grabbed a tissue from her end table, wiping her face.

"Don't worry about us. As far as we're concerned, we've already lost them. They weren't who they pretended to be. Maybe someday we'll forgive them, but maybe we won't. Either way, it's not about us. You have the ability to get justice for what they did to you, Nova, and we won't blame you if you take it. Besides, even if you don't, you aren't the only woman they've done this to."

"What?" Her gaze shot to Quinn.

"Eight women total," Quinn answered. "That's what my parents told us. If there's a chance we can get their names, we'll tell them the truth, too. Like we have you. I can't, won't, hold onto their secrets. Not when they've hurt so many people."

"What about my non-disclosure? Can I even say anything?"

"I don't know," Jesse said honestly. "I don't know how any of it works, but if you want justice, Nova, we'll get it for you. Even if we have to go to the police for you. And, even if you choose to do nothing with this information, like Quinn said, if we can find the other women, there's still a chance it will get out."

"We'd rather it be you. You—us—we started it all,"

Quinn said. "So, you need to fight back. For the baby you're having now, for me, but most importantly for you. You can sue the hospital, make enough money to set yourself up. You deserve it, Nova, after everything they put you through."

"Suing the hospital would hurt you, too. Both of you. That's your job we're talking about. Innocent people would suffer."

Jesse nodded. "We realize that, but we'd find a way to be okay. We can figure it out. There are plenty of jobs out there in our field. Ultimately, the decision is yours to make. The only person you should think about is yourself in making it. We'll support whatever you choose."

She smiled sadly, brushing a piece of hair back behind her ear. "I don't know what I'm feeling right now. I'm furious and sick to my stomach because of how unfair this all is. And I'm sad for all that I'll never get to know about you," she told Quinn, "but I can't help being overjoyed because you're...you're here. Alive. I must've pictured you a thousand times, who you would've been. But, here you are. I can't...it just doesn't feel real yet. I love you so much and yet, we're complete strangers." She rubbed her lips together, squinting her eyes.

"I know," Quinn said. "My parents still feel like my parents. My reality has been completely thrown off its axis."

"What will you two do?" Nova asked.

"Neither of us know yet. It's still fresh," Jesse answered.

She nodded. "You're both such strong kids. You're

good people. Whether that's because of your parents or in spite of them, I don't know, but if I mess with their lives, I'm messing with yours, too. I won't make my decision lightly."

"Take time, don't take time. We're behind you whatever you decide," Jesse assured her. "Just remember, your stress affects the baby. Your c-section puts you at a higher risk for complications, so if you need anything, just know that I'm here. Just like I told you before."

"Both of you?" she asked, eyeing Quinn.

"I mean, I'm not going to start calling you my mom or anything, but this relationship is growing more complicated by the second. I think we're stuck with each other." Quinn leaned forward, resting her elbows onto her knees, reaching for Jesse's hand.

"Why don't we just start with calling me a friend then?" Nova asked, tears forming in her eyes once more, though a smile was on her face.

Quinn nodded, wiping away a quick tear. "I can probably do that."

FORTY-SIX

JESSE
FIVE MONTHS LATER

Jesse raced out of the room, searching for Quinn with tears in his eyes. She stood up as she saw him, her face full of worry.

"It's a girl," he told her, running a hand over his head. "She's beautiful."

She hurried toward him, throwing her arms around his neck and planting a kiss on his lips. "Congratulations, *Dad*." She kissed him again. "How are they?"

"Both are completely healthy," he said, heaving a sigh of relief. "Nova was amazing. And the baby is...oh my god. She's gorgeous, Quinn. Seven pounds, two ounces of perfection."

"Nova's okay, then? No complications?" she asked. Jesse couldn't help but smile. Over the past few months he'd watched the two most important women in his life grow closer. He loved seeing their relationship evolve. Quinn was coming to terms with the idea of raising her, as she liked to call her, 'sister-step-daughter' with him, and Nova hadn't mentioned her feelings for Jesse since Quinn's identity had been revealed.

"She's fine. Perfect, actually. The c-section was just a precaution."

She nodded, her expression warming. "When can I see them?"

"They're letting them have a golden hour right now. Time for her to bond with Nova, but they'll let us back in once the hour's up."

She smiled. "How are you feeling? You holding up okay?"

"It's the most amazing feeling I've ever had, Quinn," he told her, his face lighting up. He couldn't conceal the smile that was burning his lips.

"I'm so proud of you." She playfully bumped his hip with hers. "*Holy cow,* you're, like, an actual parent now."

He brushed a piece of hair from her eyes, kissing her forehead. "I couldn't have done this without you."

"Well, you did *some* of it without me," she teased.

"But, I want to do the rest of it with you," he said seriously. Her reaction to anything serious was to make a joke, but this time he wouldn't let her.

She looked up at him. "Me too." He kissed her again, his arms wrapping around her, pulling her into him.

When they broke apart, he looked around, taking her hand and walking toward the vending machine. "So, this place isn't so bad, huh?"

"Atlanta? Or the hospital?"

"Both," he said with a shrug. "We'll settle in here okay. The people seem nice enough."

She nodded. "It's different than home, that's for sure, but then again, that's probably exactly what we need."

He kissed her hand, their fingers laced together. "New beginnings."

It had been three months since Nova had made the decision to press charges against their parents, and one month since the 'Dale Six,' as they'd been dubbed, had landed in jail. They were awaiting sentencing, but Jesse suspected it would be a long time before they saw any of them again. He wasn't sure how he felt about it. Deep down, he knew he'd always pictured this moment surrounded by his parents—but somehow he wasn't missing them. What they'd done was despicable, and he'd come to accept that he may never truly forgive them.

Quinn was his family now. She was the one he would build a life with, hours away from the town that had surrounded them with so much darkness and heartache. Atlanta was a chance for a new start, and they'd do it together, just like they'd done everything else throughout their lives.

Of the eight women, they'd located four total, including Nova. They were all joining her in a lawsuit against the hospital. They would win, Jesse was sure, and it might be the thing to shut down the small hospital for good. Even if it didn't, Jesse wanted nothing to do with the place, and Quinn had agreed. Within the next few weeks, they'd be moving to their new home and taking jobs with even better salaries in a place where no one knew their parents or their story. It was the freest he'd ever felt.

Dakota, the town where Nova lived, was only a little over an hour's drive from their new apartment, so he'd be able to see her and the baby often.

"Jesse," Quinn said, stopping in her tracks and nodding in the direction of the double doors. He looked over and gasped. Reagan and Gunner were standing in the doorway, Nora in Gunner's arms and a small bundle in Reagan's.

Jesse stood frozen as Reagan rushed to him, wrapping him in a hug. Jesse hugged her back, surprised and relieved not to feel the sting of jealousy he once had around Gunner.

"What are you doing here?" he asked.

"You think we weren't going to come see your baby?" Reagan asked, her smile wide and genuine. "I'm so happy for you, Jesse."

"Jesse," Nora called, leaping down from Gunner's arms and into Jesse's. He picked her up, hugging her tightly. He was surprised by how much she'd grown.

"I just can't believe you're here," he said. "Thank you, I mean. Thank you for coming. It means so much to me."

"Has she had it?" she asked.

"Yes," he said proudly, "a healthy baby girl."

"Nora will be so thrilled. A little cousin to play with," Reagan squealed. Jesse looked to Quinn, whose cheeks were growing slightly pink. She had chosen not to tell Gunner the truth about their relationship. Neither of them could know if Gunner knew about his father's affair and Quinn claimed she didn't want to ruin his perception of his father if she didn't have to. Jesse suspected she was also scared of Gunner's reaction. He knew she couldn't take losing anyone else in her life, and to keep it a secret was safer for her heart. He hoped one day he could change her mind.

Gunner approached him, shaking his hand. "Congratulations, man. We're thrilled for you."

"And you guys, too," Jesse said. "Look at this little cutie."

"This is Duncan," Reagan said proudly, leaning him forward so Jesse and Quinn could get a better look. "What have you named your little one?"

"Oh," Jesse said, realizing he hadn't even told Quinn what they'd decided on. "It's Emalee. Emalee Hope Mathis." He could tell her later that it was the name Nova would've used on her if given the chance.

He placed a finger in Duncan's tiny palm, smiling down at the precious baby.

Nora smiled at him. "He's my baby brother," she told him.

"I know," Jesse whispered. "He's perfect. I'll bet you're the best big sister."

"Momma says so," Nora agreed.

"Nora, remember Daddy and I told you Jesse was going to have a baby? There's a new little girl in our family," Reagan said, staring at her daughter. "Isn't that exciting?"

"Family?" Jesse asked. It was the second time they'd called him and Emalee their family.

"Of course, we're family, crazy. Don't think you're getting rid of me that easy," Reagan told him with a wink.

Nora wrapped her hands around his neck once again. "Do I get to meet her? I'm very good with babies."

"Of course." His heart was so full, surrounded by a family he hadn't realized he still had.

"How did you even know we were here?" Jesse asked, the thought hitting him.

"Quinn called us," Reagan explained.

"You did?" he asked, facing Quinn.

She looked down, embarrassed. "I knew you'd want your parents to be here, so when they couldn't, I didn't want you to feel like you didn't have family around to celebrate. You deserve a celebration, Jess."

His face grew warm as he smiled at her, setting Nora down. "You're always looking out for me."

She smiled. "What else are best friend-slash-girlfriends for?"

Before he could say anything, a nurse called his name from behind him. He turned around.

"Which of you is Quinn?" she asked the group. Quinn raised her hand awkwardly. "She's asking for you both."

Jesse lowered his brow, taking Quinn's hand. The hour wasn't over yet. "Will y'all stay? I'd love for you to meet her."

"Of course," Reagan said. "I'm gonna have to nurse Duncan anyway. We'll be here. No rush."

With that reassurance, he headed down the hall. He opened the door to her room. "Nova?" he called.

"Come in." She was reclined back in the bed, the baby nestled in her arms. She had small tears in her tired eyes.

"Is everything all right?" Jesse asked, hurrying to her side.

"Everything's fine," she said, keeping her voice low. "Emalee just wanted to meet her momma."

"What?" Quinn and Jesse asked at once.

Emalee stirred and Nova began to bounce her softly, tears pouring down her cheeks as she nodded.

"No," Quinn said, "*no*."

"Quinn, I'm too old to give her the life she needs. The life she deserves. She should go to you. You both. I want you to raise her together. All I ever wanted for you was a good life with a happy home. You can give Emalee that. I'll be nearly seventy when she turns eighteen. What can I do for her?"

"You can *love* her. You do love her. She needs you," Quinn said, already openly sobbing.

Nova remained calm despite her own tears. "All her life all she'll hear is 'mommy can't get down and color with you because her hips hurt' or 'mommy can't read to you because my eyesight is slipping and I've misplaced my glasses again' or 'mommy's too tired to play with you today.' What kind of a life would that be for her?"

Jesse ran a finger over Emalee's cheek. "Nova, look at what you've done, though. Despite all the worry over your age, you brought a perfectly healthy baby into this world. You can raise her. You *deserve* to raise her. And we'll be there to help whenever you need us."

"Maybe I do deserve her, but she deserves better than what I can give her at this point in my life. Now, I'm not saying I don't want to be in her life, of course I do. And I will. As a grandma or a crazy aunt, whatever you think is best. But, you two can give her a life I can only dream of giving her. You can afford things I never will. She can go after her dreams with you, move mountains if she chooses."

"Money isn't everything, Nova," Jesse said softly.

"I'm not only talking about money, Jesse. I'm talking about a childhood to remember. Not having to feel like she can't go out with her friends because I'm old and sick and she thinks she should have to take care of me. I'm talking about two parents—together and in love. Two parents who dance together in the kitchen after the kids have gone to bed or who laugh together at the dinner table. Seems like such a silly thing, but when I was growing up, being shipped from foster home to foster home, all I wanted was to find a home with a mom and a dad who loved me...and loved each other just as much." She laughed through her tears. "Okay, maybe I wanted a dog, too. My point is, you can give Emalee all that I want to give her but can't."

Jesse looked to Quinn, whose cheeks were shiny with tears. "I don't know if I'm ready," she whispered, looking at him wildly.

"You are," Nova answered for him. "You both are."

Jesse bent down beside the bed, looking Nova in the

eye. "Are you sure about this? Maybe you should take some more time to think. This is such a huge decision."

"No, I'm sure. If I take more time, I'll change my mind, but that would be for me, not her. I want to make this decision selflessly."

He wrapped his hand around her arm, tears flowing from every eye in the room. "It just doesn't feel fair. You love her so much."

"It's *because* I love her I can do this." She kissed the baby's pink forehead. "I told you this story wouldn't have a happy ending. Not for me anyway. But it can for her. And for you," she said, looking at Quinn. "That's all I've ever really wanted." She reached up, wiping tears away from her eyes.

Quinn stepped forward, bending down beside Jesse and placing her hand on Nova's leg. "Can I hold her?" she asked.

"Of course," Nova said, seeming surprised. Quinn held out her arms, standing back up and taking Emalee into her arms. Jesse stood up beside her, placing one hand on the small of her back and the other on the baby in her arms.

"She's beautiful, isn't she?"

Quinn nodded quickly, a toothy grin on her face. "Just like our mother." She looked at Nova. It was the first time Jesse had heard her say the word in reference to Novalee.

"So, what do you think?" he asked, kissing the side of her head. "Are you in?"

Nova was watching them, a warm smile on her face

despite the tears that hadn't stopped. Quinn nodded at her before looking to him. "I'm in, Jess. Of course I'm in." Jesse kissed her forehead and then Emalee's, his chest swelling with pride. "But, if you change your mind—" she started, looking at Nova again.

"I won't," Nova assured them. "But, I do have one request."

"Okay, anything," Jesse responded.

"I want you two to get married."

"Married?" Quinn said a bit too loudly, startling Emalee. The infant began fussing in her arms and Quinn bent her knees, bouncing carefully in an attempt to calm her.

"Yes. Emalee deserves parents with the same last name as her." She nodded, her face serious. "Another dream of mine. You'd be surprised how much that matters to a little girl who feels like she has no one else like her in the world."

Jesse looked to Quinn, a smirk on his face. "I mean, eventually we will," Quinn said.

"Yeah," he agreed. "Eventually." He reached into his pocket, where the ring had been burning a hole in his pocket for months. *It was too soon,* he'd convinced himself. He wanted to wait until they'd been dating for at least a year. Quinn was known to run at the first sign of commitment, and he was terrified of scaring her off. He pulled it out anyway, showing her the box. "Or, now?"

Her eyes lit up. "Oh my."

"Well?" he asked, leaning down on one knee. "Will

you marry me, Quinn? Will you be my best friend-girl-friend-mother of my child-wife for the rest of our lives?"

She laughed. "Well, we do have two witnesses here today." She raised an eyebrow. "Maybe we could convince them to stick around for a day until we can get everything ready."

"Are you serious?" Jesse gulped, hopping to his feet.

Quinn blushed. "I mean, it's too soon, right?"

"It could never be too soon with you, Quinn." He took the ring out of the box, holding out his hand for hers.

She went pale. "You're really serious?"

"I've never been more serious in my life. I love you more than anything. You've been my best friend, the one I can count on, through every crazy thing I've gone through. When I look back on my life, there you are. It's always been you, Quinn. It's always been us."

"You've had this ring for how long?" She stared at it suspiciously.

"I bought it after I found you in that basement. I realized then I never wanted to go another day without you. Losing you would be losing a piece of myself. Quinn, you told me once that we were like a city skyline—beautiful and perfect from a distance but messy and complicated up close. And, quite honestly, you were right. We are messy. And we are complicated. But, I'd rather have a messy, complicated life with you than a perfect one with anyone else."

She kissed him over the baby, their lips mashing together and warming him to his core. "Me, too," she whispered, her lips still brushing his.

"Yeah?" He pulled away, a smile filling his face.

She laughed through her happy tears. "Yeah. Of course. You're it for me, Jesse Mathis. You have been for as long as I can remember."

"Then why not? Who cares if it's too soon? Who cares if it isn't what we envisioned?" He touched Emalee's forehead. "Nothing about our life is what we planned, but I wouldn't change a single thing. Complicated looks good on us." He winked at her, his heart pounded as he stared at his best friend, the mother of his child, and the woman he planned to love for the rest of his life.

"Okay," she told him, raising her arms to brush her cheek against Emalee's.

"Okay?" he asked, an eyebrow raised.

"Yes, Jesse. Let's get married." Her smile grew. He kissed her again, his hands in her hair as he leaned over the baby. "But, we have to wait."

"Wait? Because you don't want it at the courthouse?" His heart plummeted, his excitement fading, replaced with disappointment.

She shook her head. "I don't care where I marry you, Jess, but I do care who's there. Reagan and Gunner, Nora, and Duncan—they're your family. But, I need mine." She smiled at Nova, moving to the bed and taking her hand. "And we need ours." She kissed Emalee's head once again. "I can't do it without her."

"Then you won't," he repeated. "Our family should be there—all of them." He walked toward Nova's bed, too, accepting that his family now looked so much different than he'd once thought it would. Yesterday, he was a man who wasn't sure he had any family left in the world, but today he was surrounded by a great, big, crazy, dysfunctional, yet somehow perfect family. A mess. His mess—one he couldn't live without.

Keep reading for a SNEAK PEEK of:

The Liar, The Messes Series Book Three

CHAPTER ONE

FLETCHER

Fletcher Denali's life began the moment that it ended. At least that's what he'd always believed...until the day he met her. From the moment he laid eyes on Vaida Williams, he knew he hadn't been living. Not really. Not yet. She was the first girl to make him look twice since Holly.

"Fletcher," Burt called from behind him, making him jump up and bang his head on the inside of the stove he'd been cleaning.

"Oh, shit, ouch. Yeah?" He spun around, clutching his head. Burt stood in front of him, next to a woman he'd never seen before. She smiled at him, her dark eyes glowing next to her caramel skin.

"Hi," he said, smiling through the radiating pain in his head. He pulled his hand away, checking to make sure there was no blood before he offered it up to the girl. She shook it cautiously.

"Fletch, this is Vaida. Vaida, Fletcher Denali. He takes care of everything around here, so if you have any questions, he's your guy. Fletcher, I want you to show her the ropes around this place."

"Okay, no problem," Fletcher agreed, throwing the grease-covered towel over his shoulder. With that, Burt walked away, leaving them alone. "Welcome to the madhouse," Fletcher joked, watching as her eyes scanned the room before landing back on him.

"That bad?" she asked, baring her teeth in a grimace.

He waved a hand. "Nah, Burt's a good boss. The rest of the guys here are pretty cool, too."

She didn't look entirely convinced as she ran a finger across the countertop. "Okay, good." She bobbed her head. "Well, put me to work."

He nodded, handing her a clean cloth from above their heads. Any of the other guys would've put her on the stove and taken the easy job for themselves, but Fletcher couldn't make himself do it. "We're in between rushes right now, so I'm just trying to clean up a bit. You can start by wiping down all the counters." He handed her a bottle of sanitizing spray.

"Okay," she said, turning and beginning to spray the stainless steel countertops. He got on his knees, stuck his head back into the oven, and began scrubbing the caked on food again. He was strangely conscious of how he looked, trying to angle himself in an attractive way though this was hardly a sexy job.

"So, are you from around here, Vaida?" he asked, his voice echoing from inside the oven.

"No," she said simply, not bothering to elaborate.

"What brings you to Burt's, then? A love of greasy food and long hours?" he teased.

"No," she said again. "I just...needed a change. My roommate knows Burt; he helped me get the job."

"Your roommate?" he asked, sliding out of the stove and wiping his hands off. "Anyone I might know?"

She was quiet for a moment. "It's a big city, Fletcher. Do you really think you know every person?" Her voice was almost cold.

"Sorry," he said, leaning back in and scrubbing away again. He'd obviously offended her somehow. Small talk had never been his forté. "I'm not trying to sound nosey. It just gets quiet around here. I'll shut up."

When she spoke again, several minutes had passed, and it almost shocked him to hear her voice. "I don't mean to be rude. I'm just...I don't like to talk about myself."

Now, that was something he at least understood. "Hey, you don't owe me an apology. I was just making small talk." He couldn't help his clipped tone.

"How long have you worked here?" she asked.

"Not too long. Just since last fall." When she didn't respond, he peeked out of the stove, watching her scrub the countertops. She was slow, methodical, and he was mesmerized by her movements. Her shoulder-length, black hair was tied in a loose ponytail at the nape of her neck. The blue jeans she wore wrapped tightly around her curves, and the black t-shirt lifted up when she leaned over too far to reveal a small sliver of her light brown skin.

She stopped moving, looking over her shoulder at him. "Am I doing something wrong?"

"What? No." He looked away quickly. "No, you're doing fine."

She nodded, her brow furrowed as if she were thinking hard. "So, are *you* from here, then? Atlanta, I mean."

"Nah," he said, catching himself before he told too much of the truth. "I'm from all over."

"Ahh, so you're an Army brat?"

"No, just a brat in general."

She let out a small laugh. "You're a funny guy, huh?"

"I do what I can," he said, a cocky grin spreading on his face. "So, have you settled in yet? Made some friends?"

"*Made some friends?* What, like we're in kindergarten?" She snorted.

"No, not really. Why? Are you offering?"

He stood up, dusting off his knees. "Well, if you insist. I'm pretty familiar with Atlanta at this point, at least. I could take you to a party, introduce you to a few people. Have you feeling right at home."

"Thanks, but I'm all right," she said, her smile sad. She looked at the cloth in her hand. "I appreciate the offer though."

"Sure, anytime." He looked down, then back up, unable to deny the disappointment he felt. "It's a standing invitation," he told her, kicking himself for sounding so desperate to get to know her.

"I'll keep that in mind," she said, starting to scrub the counter again. "Thanks, Fletcher."

He nodded, trying to stop staring at her, though it was growing increasingly difficult to pull his eyes away.

Ready to read more? The Liar, The Messes Series Book Three is available now!

LOVED THE HEALER?

Thank you so much for reading The Healer! If you enjoyed it, I would love for you to check out the rest of The Messes Series.

The Cleaner—Gunner's story
The Liar—Fletcher's story
The Prisoner—Fiona's story

It is extremely important that the rest of the series be read in order.

If you enjoy them, I humbly ask that you leave a review on the platform where you purchased this copy. I would appreciate it so much!

Thanks for reading!

XO,

Kiersten Modglin

ACKNOWLEDGMENTS

Thank you so much for reading the second book in The Messes Series: The Healer.

I hope you enjoyed Jesse and Quinn's story as much as I enjoyed bringing it to life. Without the help of so many amazing people, this book wouldn't have been possible.

First and foremost, to *my amazing husband*, for always being so supportive of this dream of mine. Thank you for loving me enough to inspire me to write about love. You are my happily ever after.

To *my PA*, Brittany, for being my sounding board and biggest fan. Jesse's story wouldn't exist without you and I'll forever be thankful for our brainstorming session that brought these characters to fruition. Thank you for cheering me on every step of the way.

To *my family*, my first readers and the ones who believed in me long before anyone knew my name, I love you all. Thank you for inspiring so many crazy characters and for raising me surrounded by books.

To *my Twisted Readers and Street Team*, you guys are my rock! I'm so thankful for our group, our crazy games, and the unending support you show me. You are amazing!

To *my betas*, Brittany, Katie, and Holly, for reading this book before it was ready to see the light of day and helping me decide what worked and what didn't. Your insights and support mean more to me than you'll ever know.

To *Janise Tedlock, Shelly Reynolds, and Diane Norwood,* readers who won a chance to make an appearance in this story, I hope you enjoyed your characters! I had so much fun bringing all three of you to life in this book. Janise, you were a strong, independent woman who helped Quinn when she desperately needed it. Shelly and Diane, your characters were brave when it mattered most and their story was so important to Jesse and Quinn's. In a way, your characters made their love a possibility. Without you, there's a good chance they would've never met. All three characters were essential to the plot and I hope you'll enjoy reading about them for years to come.

To *my editor*, Sarah West from Three Owls Editing, thank you for whipping this book into shape. Jesse and Quinn deserve the best and you are it!

To *everyone who read and loved The Cleaner and asked me to make Gunner's story into a series,* thank you from the bottom of my heart! I am still in awe of what an impact these stories have made on my readers, and without you, your support, and your outstanding reactions to The Cleaner, the rest of this series would have never existed. I hope this book lived up to your expectations.

And lastly, *to everyone who read and enjoyed this story*, thank you for supporting me.

I truly hope this story meant something to you. Whether it was a good laugh or an ugly cry, I hope it made you feel. After all, that's what art is all about. If this is your first experience with one of my books, I hope you'll hurry to read my others. If this is just one of the many of my books that you've read, thank you for reading again! I hope this book was everything you've come to expect from my books and a total surprise all at once.

ABOUT THE AUTHOR

KIERSTEN MODGLIN is an Amazon Top 10 bestselling author of psychological thrillers and a member of International Thriller Writers, Novelists, Inc., and the Alliance of Independent Authors. Kiersten is a KDP Select All-Star and a recipient of *ThrillerFix*'s Best Psychological Thriller Award, *Suspense Magazine*'s Best Book of 2021 Award, a 2022 Silver Falchion for Best Suspense, and a 2022 Silver Falchion for Best Overall Book of 2021. She grew up in rural western Kentucky and later relocated to Nashville, Tennessee, where she now lives with her husband, daughter, and their two Boston terriers: Cedric and Georgie. Kiersten's work is currently being translated into multiple languages and readers across the world refer to her as 'The Queen of Twists.' A Netflix addict, Shonda Rhimes superfan, psychology fanatic, and *indoor* enthusiast, Kiersten enjoys rainy days spent with her nose in a book.

Sign up for Kiersten's newsletter here:
kierstenmodglinauthor.com/nlsignup

Sign up for text alerts from Kiersten here:
kierstenmodglinauthor.com/textalerts

kierstenmodglinauthor.com
www.facebook.com/kierstenmodglinauthor
www.facebook.com/groups/kmodsquad
www.twitter.com/kmodglinauthor
www.instagram.com/kierstenmodglinauthor
www.tiktok.com/@kierstenmodglinauthor
www.goodreads.com/kierstenmodglinauthor
www.bookbub.com/authors/kiersten-modglin
www.amazon.com/author/kierstenmodglin

ALSO BY KIERSTEN MODGLIN

STANDALONE NOVELS

Widow Falls

Missing Daughter

The Reunion

Tell Me the Truth

The Dinner Guests

If You're Reading This...

A Quiet Retreat

ARRANGEMENT TRILOGY

The Arrangement (Book 1)

The Amendment (Book 2)

The Atonement (Book 3)

THE MESSES SERIES

The Cleaner (The Messes, #1)

The Healer (The Messes, #2)

The Liar (The Messes, #3)

The Prisoner (The Messes, #4)

NOVELLAS

The Long Route: A Lover's Landing Novella

The Stranger in the Woods: A Crimson Falls Novella

45101202R00162